"I'll bet you it won't be long before someone writes a song about the Groover kid and how heroic he was at Guadalcanal. That's what they did for some guy named Roger Young, on account of his actions on the island of New Georgia in the Solomons. The song 'Comin' in on a Wing and a Prayer' was also a true story."

"Propaganda."

"Wait a minute. Are you telling me those songs aren't true?"

"They're true, but they're embellished. Right now the country's crazy over heroes, but once the people wake up to the fact that thousands of men won't be coming home, the reality of the war is going to hit home. And hit hard. In the meantime you and I have the unpleasant task of keeping order while laurels are heaped on an accomplice in a still-unsolved crime."

**Return to the homefront
in these other Kate Fallon mysteries
by M. T. Jefferson . . .**

In the Mood for Murder

The Victory Dance Murder

MORE MYSTERIES FROM THE
BERKLEY PUBLISHING GROUP . . .

Decorated for
Murder

M. T. Jefferson

BERKLEY PRIME CRIME, NEW YORK

DECORATED FOR MURDER

A Berkley Prime Crime Book / published by arrangement with the author

PRINTING HISTORY
Berkley Prime Crime mass-market edition / July 2002

Copyright © 2002 by H. Paul Jeffers.
Cover art by Charles Pyle.

Visit our website at
www.penguinputnam.com

ISBN: 0-425-18224-X

Berkley Prime Crime Books are published
by The Berkley Publishing Group,
a division of Penguin Putnam Inc.,
375 Hudson Street, New York, New York 10014.
The name BERKLEY PRIME CRIME and
the BERKLEY PRIME CRIME design
are trademarks belonging to Penguin Putnam Inc.

PRINTED IN THE UNITED STATES OF AMERICA

10 9 8 7 6 5 4 3 2 1

The Assignment

WHEN A STACK of brittle, brownish-yellow, musty-smelling old editions of the Robinsville *Independence* landed on my desk with a dull thump, the top paper of the bundle was dated January 14, 1943. It had a banner headline: SHOCKING DEATH OF OUR WAR HERO.

Beneath it in smaller type was:

Body of Sgt. John Groover Found at Washington Field;
War Hero Was 1941 All-Star of County Pigskin League
May Have Died from Complications of Wounds
Suffered at Guadalcanal; He was Slated to Receive
Congressional Medal of Honor from
President Roosevelt

Looking up from the paper, I found my boss looking down at me. Short and plump with thinning reddish hair and a nose that seemed to have been broken more than once, Paul Fallon was the paper's editor-in-chief. He had been doing the job for more than three decades.

For reasons known only to him, he had hired me straight out of Temple University's Journalism School with the promise that if I proved I could "cut the mustard," as he'd put it to me on that nervous day, he might take me on as a reporter. In the meantime I would get the routine stuff, such as writing obituaries for the files of prominent townspeople who were still alive, covering school board meetings, and reporting on the socially important weddings and births.

A couple of months later I was assigned to features. I handled "Robinsville Citizen of the Month," "Our Teacher of the Year," and "This Date in Robinsville History."

During my job interview, I'd informed Paul that my long-term journalistic goal was to be a crime reporter. Now, here he was tapping a stubby finger on the headline in an almost sixty-year-old *Independence* and saying, "Here's your big chance. What you'll find in these papers is a mystery without a solution. I say it was a case of murder. I expect you to prove I'm right."

With a puzzled look that darted from his face to the stack of papers and back to him, I blurted out, "Who could possibly care now?"

He came up straight. "Me. Go through those papers and you'll understand why."

Four paragraphs down in a story written by Augustus MacFarland, the editor whom Paul Fallon had succeeded in the late 1970s, I found a possible explanation for my boss's interest in having me dig into an event that had taken place four decades before I was even a gleam in my parents' eyes and when Paul Fallon must have been a kid. I read:

> The body of the war hero was discovered by two youths on their way to classes at Robinsville High School. Taking a shortcut across the gridiron on which Johnny Groover had been a star quarterback, they noticed what they thought was a drunken man lying in the middle of the playing field. When they saw that it was Johnny Groover, and realized he was dead, they ran to the nearby field house to report the discovery to Robinsville High's football coach, Ralph Franklin, who called the police.
>
> A few hours before his death Groover had been feted at a reception that was organized by Miss Kate Fallon and Mrs. Beatrice Bradshaw.

Laying down the fragile newspaper, I shouted across the city room, "Hey, boss, the Kate Fallon in this story, is she any relation to—"

"Kate was my sister. She died ten years ago. Everybody whose name you'll find in those stories is gone. The police chief, coroner, Groover's football coach, classmates, all the figures in the case are dead . . . except one. Scrappy MacFarland is still with us. He must be getting close to a hundred years old. But he's still got the old spark that made him the greatest newsman I've ever known. Scrappy knows everything that happened in the Groover case, including why it was never officially listed in police files as a murder case. I have been trying for fifty years to get him to open up about it, but he'd just sit there like a chubby gnome, his lips sealed."

Tilting back in my chair and drumming fingers on the stack of old papers, I asked, "What makes you think Mr. MacFarland—"

"Good lord, kid, when you talk to him, don't call him that. If you address him as mister, he'll boot you out. He's always been called Scrappy."

"If he never opened up to you about this story," I said, "why should he suddenly want to talk to me?"

"In spite of Scrappy's carefully cultivated image of the curmudgeon, he's a softie deep down in his heart. If you tell him that you'll get fired if you don't get the truth of who killed Johnny Groover—and why, and how come it's been covered up all this time—I'm confident that he'll spill the beans."

With a nervous smile, I asked, "You wouldn't really fire me if I don't get the true story, would you? That's a bluff to get Scrappy to open up about this case, right?"

"Maybe. Or maybe not. I'll just say this about what I've learned about the news game, kid. When you're chasing a story, you're a fool if you don't understand that every minute of every day you're just an inch away from your boss saying to you, 'Here's your hat, don't let the door smack you in the ass on your way out.' You'll find Scrappy out at the Manor Retirement Home, where he spends the day flirting with the nurses. The best way to get on his good side is to take along a couple of Macanudo cigars. He prefers Lonsdales."

Before going to see MacFarland, I read all the stories about Johnny Groover in the old papers. Someone once said that journalism is the first draft of history. Turning the delicate half-century-old pages of the *Independence*, I found myself drawn back to a small Pennsylvania steel town doing its best to cope with a world turned upside down. Before that day, the Second World War for me had been grainy, black-and-white images in History Channel documentaries. The people on the screen seemed as far away from me in time as knights in shining armor. But scanning the headlines and reading stories of the war in the old papers, I discovered ordinary people not only trying to cope with the horrors of distant battles, but dreading telegrams arriving from someone in the War Department about boys who would never be coming home. There were shortages of food, no gas for their cars, scrap metal collections, paper drives, ration stamps, and the hospital the Army had built on the outskirts of Robinsville that was handling a steady stream of the wounded, crippled, and blinded young men who arrived nearly every day on the Reading Railroad.

As I drove to the Manor Retirement Home to interview Scrappy MacFarland in the hope of finding the who and whys of the mysterious death of Sergeant Johnny Groover of the United States Marine Corps and hero of the battle for Guadalcanal, the railway station was long-since gone, victim of the postwar boom in automobiles and superhighways. The George Washington Army Hospital was now the campus of a small Christian college. And the people whose names I'd read in the old papers were buried in Morris Cemetery . . . except one.

Entering Scrappy MacFarland's private, comfortable-looking room, I could not help comparing the scene to one in the movie *Citizen Kane* in which a reporter for a newsreel came to talk with the character played by Joseph Cotten. It also took place in a nursing home, although Joseph Cotten was a gray-haired, slender, frail-looking figure bundled up in a thick white robe. Scrappy MacFarland was a fat man with unruly brown hair without a strand of gray in it. He was wearing an open brown Harris tweed jacket, a scarlet ascot tucked into an open white shirt, and charcoal gray slacks. If I hadn't known his age, I would have taken him for no older than sixty-five or seventy. Seated in a pool of sunlight in a commodious overstuffed armchair, he greeted me with a challenging look and demanded, "What did you say your name was on the phone?"

"I told you on the phone that my name was M. T. Jefferson. It still is."

There was a flicker of a smile. "Correction! I should have said, 'On the phone, what did you say your name was?' What can I do for you, Mr. M. T. Jefferson?"

Taking two cellophane-wrapped Macanudo Lonsdales from my pocket and handing them to him, I said, "Everyone calls me Jeff."

Head down, he studied the cigars as if they were priceless objects as he said, "You've come to ask me about Johnny Groover."

I sat on a corner of his neatly made bed. "Why do you think I'm here about him?"

"As regular as clockwork every year," Scrappy replied as he carefully stripped a cigar of cellophane, "Paulie Fallon sends a new man out to see me in the hope that he can succeed on a mission in which all his predecessors failed. Paulie always tells them to bring me cigars."

"Is that why you haven't talked about Groover all this time, to keep the cigars coming?"

He sniffed the Macanudo. "The stogies are nice, but it's the visiting that I like."

"Surely, other people come to see you?"

"The trouble with getting to be my age is that you eventually run out of all the people you know." Then came a slow lighting process. It involved wetting the end of the cigar, clipping it with a brass cutter taken from a pocket, striking a long wooden match taken from a box of them from another pocket, drawing in the smoke, and letting it flow out in a long plume. "When I first came to this town back in the 1930s," he continued thoughtfully, "the Morris Cemetery had half its present occupancy. Most of the additions were friends of mine. There are also a few there who thought they were my enemies."

"My boss believes Groover was murdered and that you helped cover it up. He says that if I don't get the true story about what happened, I'll be fired."

He moved to the window and stood looking out, smoking all the time.

"I know the what, where, and when concerning Groover's death from your articles in the newspaper," I said. "What's missing is how he died and why it was so important that the public not be told the truth."

Turning with the long cigar jutting from a corner of his mouth, he talked around it. "There was a war on."

"It ended more than half a century ago."

He returned to his chair. "What do you know about the Marines on Guadalcanal?"

"Not much."

Holding the cigar at arm's length, he said, "That's the trouble with your generation. You all believe that history begins with your birthday. Well, young man, I'm going to tell you about Guadalcanal, because it's there that your story about Johnny Groover must begin."

I bolted off the bed. "You're going to tell me what happened?"

He looked at me with a mischievous half smile. "Yeah, I'm gonna save your job. As you said, it's been fifty years. Everyone who knew about Johnny Groover is long dead, except me, so who is there that could be hurt now if it all comes out? When I'm done, you'll know everything. Then it will be up to you whether Paulie Fallon goes to press with the whole sad story."

Grinning like a kid on Christmas morning, I blurted out, "This is great!"

"This will take a while."

"I'll give you all the time you need."

"Only the Almighty can do that, kid."

— Part 1 —

Going Back

You'd be so nice to come home to.

—Song lyric, 1943

1

IN THE STIFLING air of a rainy September night on the fetid jungle island of Guadalcanal in the Solomon Islands, Corporal Johnny Groover and Private Billy Lee Austin, B Company, Third Battalion, Fifth Division, U.S. Marines, were dug in on a ridge about a mile south of a captured Japanese airfield. They found themselves there because the landing strip had been designated the main objective of the war's first landing by United States forces on territory captured by the Japanese soon after they bombed Pearl Harbor. The U.S. Pacific Fleet commander Admiral Chester Nimitz had ordered the tiny islands of the Solomon chain taken to provide bases for the Navy to guard transport ships ferrying guns and fresh troops from Hawaii to General Douglas MacArthur's army in Australia. From the captured airstrip on Guadalcanal, Navy planes would also bomb big Japanese air and sea bases at Rabaul on the island of New Britain.

Johnny, Billy Lee, and thousands of Marines in the First Division had boarded landing craft on the seventh of August and swarmed ashore only to find the enemy had fled into the jungle. Boasted one lieutenant of the "Canal" landings, "This was a nice show. It was like takin' a freakin' piece of candy from a baby."

Five days later, a captured Japanese had led that lieutenant and a patrol of twenty-five Marines, including Johnny and Billy Lee, down a trail toward a village where the prisoner said a small group of Japanese were waiting to surrender. When the patrol approached the village, a machine gun opened up, killing the lieutenant and the prisoner. As the patrol scattered, snipers firing on them from trees killed or gravely wounded all but five of the Americans. With his right arm slightly grazed, Johnny returned fire as Billy Lee and the others dashed to a lagoon and swam for their lives. Following them, Johnny prayed, "God, if you get me out of this, I promise I'll change my ways and make up for all the bad I've done." Out of range of bullets on the other side, he looked back to see Japanese soldiers bayoneting the wounded Marines. As his wounded arm was treated at his base, another lieutenant informed him that he would be recommended for a Purple Heart. "If you'd been hit a little worse," he added, "you'd be on your way home."

"Maybe so," said Johnny, "but I just thank God I'm alive."

Arm bandaged, he was issued a replacement for the M-1 Garand rifle he'd lost while he swam the lagoon and returned to his unit. With the airstrip taken and named Henderson Field, the Japanese on August twenty-first launched a series of counterattacks across the Tenaru

River. Assisting in wiping them out, he was shot again, this time in the right thigh. Not serious enough to render him unable to return to combat duty, the wound earned him a second Purple Heart.

Back with his company, he found himself face-to-face with the company commander as the captain demanded, "What's with you, Groover? First, you get winged in the arm. Now it's the leg. What are you, some kind of biological freak that makes you a magnet for Jap bullets? Or is it that you don't like the way I run this outfit? Do you figure that if you get shot up enough, you can get transferred out from under me?"

"No, sir," Johnny exclaimed. "There's no one I'd rather serve under than you, sir. It was God that got me through every time."

"Well, son, I can't think of anybody I'd rather have serving under me than a man who's on good terms with the Lord," said the captain. "But do try a little bit harder to dodge those Jap bullets. We've got a long road ahead of us before we get to Tokyo and then go home."

Declared sufficiently fit to fight on September tenth, Johnny joined Billy Lee Austin and B Company at the east end of a long curved ridge with smaller hills trailing off at various points like legs of some giant centipede. Oriented north and south, the ridge stretched for two miles from the Pacific into the jungle and provided a superb defensive position should the Japanese attempt to land troops in an effort to recapture the airfield. After two nights of air attacks launched from Rabaul, the attack began just past nightfall on September thirteenth.

Around noontime as a horde of Japanese poured from the jungle, the blast of a mortar shell took off Billy Lee's head as he manned a machine gun. Spattered with Billy Lee's blood and bits of his flesh, Johnny grabbed the machine gun and fired it while praying it would not run out of ammunition. The fighting raged for two days with a dozen Japanese attacks repulsed. Already being called the "Battle of Bloody Ridge," it ended with more than two thousand enemies killed. Among them were 200 mowed down by Billy Lee Austin's machine gun in Johnny's hands. The Marines lost 31 men, with 9 listed as missing in action, and 103 wounded. Wounded in the upper left chest, Johnny was treated by a medic on the spot, then evacuated to a field hospital and taken to a hospital ship for surgery to remove the bullet.

Four days later he found himself looking up from a hospital bed in Australia and into the face of a Navy lieutenant junior grade. Solidly built with thick, curly black hair and brown eyes, the officer smiled broadly as he said, "This third wound was a charm. You'll soon be going home a certified hero."

Johnny frowned. "Home? I'd rather not."

The lieutenant jg's smile faded. "No one's asking you what you want. Nobody gives a damn what you may want. When the United States government says you're a hero and you're going home, you don't argue. At this very moment, the brass hats back in Washington are busy putting out the word to the whole country that Sergeant John Groover is the biggest damn deal in a Yank uniform since Sergeant Alvin York in the First World War."

"Excuse me, but it's *Corporal* Groover."

"As of yesterday, you're promoted. But getting three stripes is just the beginning. I have orders that say as soon as you're able to stand on your feet, I'm to escort you to

Hawaii and then on to a hospital in Frisco. Once you're fully recovered, you are going to be the star attraction on a national tour to sell War Bonds. At some point you will report in your dress uniform to the White House, where the president will pin on your chest every decoration and medal available, including the Congressional Medal of Honor."

Johnny barked a laugh that hurt his tightly bandaged ribs. "Ah, now I get it! One of the clowns in my old outfit put you up to this, right? You're not an officer. You ought to be an actor in the movies. So who the hell are you?"

"I'm Dino Minetta, United States Navy Office of Public Information. I've been detached temporarily from Pearl Harbor to deliver your wisecracking ass stateside at the earliest possible moment. The American people are hungry for a hero and you've been picked."

Johnny winced. "Whose bright idea was that?"

"The order came directly from the commander in chief. President Roosevelt heard about you from his favorite commentator on the radio. His name is Alexander Whiteside and I gather he's a friend of FDR who often stays at the White House. When Whiteside learned about your exploits from someone in the Navy Department, he went on the air and told the whole country about them. Thanks to him you'll be getting the red carpet treatment. When you arrive in your hometown, they'll probably march out the high school band and a bevy of swooning, pom-pom-waving cheerleaders to meet you at the railroad station, if there is one in that burg."

"Look, Lieutenant," said Johnny with a worried expression, "this is a huge mistake. The reason I'm in the

Marines is that a judge in my hometown gave me the choice of joining up or sitting in a prison cell."

The officer's grin reappeared. "The American people *love* yarns about bad boys who turn out good! Huckleberry Finn! Peck's Bad Boy. The tough kid Mickey Rooney played in the movie *Boys' Town*. The East Side kids! Just what did you to do to get on the wrong side of the law, stick up an ice cream truck?"

"Actually, it was an armored car carrying fifty thousand dollars in payroll for the town's steel plant."

"You robbed a fifty-grand payroll and didn't get prison time?"

"I was just the lookout, so when I came before the judge, he took pity on me on account of my age. Also, my dad pleaded for leniency. Dad is the judge's milkman."

Minetta laughed. "God bless the American small town!"

"Speaking of God, is there a chaplain around here that I could talk to?"

"The hospital's got three, actually. Which do you prefer, minister, priest, or rabbi?"

"For all that I've done, I should probably see all of them."

"If your conscience is troubled by the two hundred Nips you gunned down, forget it. The sonsabitches died happy to be able to join their glorious ancestors."

"They don't bother me a bit. I'm thinking about bad stuff I did before the war."

2

IN THE EARLY hours of the morning of Wednesday, December thirty-first, Scrappy MacFarland, the fat, balding editor of the daily Robinsville, Pennsylvania, *Independence,* used one sausagelike finger of each hand to attack the keys of a black, clanky Underwood typewriter. The resulting sound in his office adjacent to the newspaper's city room was a rapid, mechanical chattering not unlike that of the Thompson automatic submachine guns in the hands of tough guys portrayed by James Cagney, George Raft, and Edward G. Robinson in a seemingly endless string of glamorized gangster films in the 1930s. As rumpled-looking as an unmade bed and with a gone-out, half-smoked La Primadora cigar clamped in the right side of his mouth, Scrappy typed a headline for the main story of the front page:

CEREMONY WILL HONOR LOCAL HERO
OF GUADALCANAL BATTLE; COMMITTEE

APPOINTED TO PLAN FESTIVITIES TO MARK
A YEAR OF PROMISING BEGINNINGS

Pausing, he plucked the cold cigar from his mouth and thought about relighting it. Before the war, this would never have crossed his mind. He would have tossed the stogie into the trash basket and lit another. In his experience, restarting a cigar that had gone out was almost as bad as reheating a pot of yesterday's coffee. But as he'd pointed out to the paper's readers in almost daily editorials throughout the past twelve months, there was a war on. A new commandment had been added to the Old Testament's ten: "Thou shalt not waste." Not food, not gasoline, not paper, not cooking grease, not rubber, not scrap metal, not silk stockings, and not anything else that in some way might help to bring the war to a swift and victorious end. In the case of cigars there were three reasons not to waste. First, tobacco had been put on a government list of products to which the military was to have priority. No American boy or man would go marching off to war without an ample supply of smokes. Second, matches used to light cigars contained sulphur, an ingredient of munitions. And they were made of paper, of which there was already such a shortage that the size of the *Independence* had been reduced from eight pages a day to four.

The cigar had come from a box of fifty La Primadoras that had been a Christmas gift from his friend Kate Fallon. Mindful of the paper shortage, she had presented the box without gift wrapping at the annual *Independence* staff Christmas party. Smoking again and aware that the men in the press room were waiting for the front-page story to accompany a photo of Johnny Groover so they could print the edition and go home, Scrappy resumed typing. He wrote:

> When the people of Robinsville salute the hero-
> ism of USMC Sergeant John Groover during the
> battle for Guadalcanal, the tribute will be held only
> thirteen months after the attack by the Japanese on
> our Pacific fleet at Pearl Harbor on a day that Pres-
> ident Roosevelt rightly defined as a date that will
> live in infamy. Who on that dark occasion would
> have dared to predict that by the end of 1942 the
> forces of freedom would be grabbing the offensive
> all over the globe?

When Scrappy paused again, reading his words, a thrilling tingle coursed down his broad back as he pondered the state of the war only six months earlier. Hitler's armies had taken all the land between the English Channel and the gates of Moscow and from Norway to Greece. His Panzer tanks had the run of French North Africa, stood poised to smash the British Army in Egypt, and threatened to grab the Suez Canal. In Asia and the Pacific, the navy and army of the Empire of Japan had swept over Malaya, Burma, the Dutch East Indies, the Philippines, the Solomon Islands, and New Guinea to stand at the doorstep of Australia. In the six months after the attack on the U.S. fleet at Pearl Harbor, the forces of "the Rising Sun" had conquered a land and sea area more than twice the size of the United States.

After considering this dismal history, Scrappy puffed cigar smoke and continued:

As you read my words, Russians are beating back the Nazis at Stalingrad. Great Britain remains free, and inspired by Churchill to give their blood, toil, tears and sweat, the great people of the United Kingdom no longer must stand alone. Under the command of General Eisenhower, GI's have liberated Morocco and Algeria in North Africa and are now engaged in battles against Hitler's vaunted tank army under General Erwin (the Desert Fox) Rommel in the desert sands of Tunisia. Egypt and the Suez Canal are no longer threatened. Half-a-world away in steamy jungles of New Guinea, outnumbered soldiers under General Douglas MacArthur have smashed a 10,000-man Japanese force, driving it off that island and ending its threat to Australia. Late in the year U.S. Marines landed at a speck of island in the Solomons known as Guadalcanal. They soon drove a Japanese garrison from an airstrip and then withstood ferocious shelling from Japanese ships and a furious counterattack. When it was over, the enemy dead were piled in stacks by the thousand.

While pockets of Emperor Hirohito's men continue to hold on, for the first time in the war Japs have been forced to give up land they thought they'd conquered as part of their plan for domination of the Pacific.

Stopping and looking at a wall clock with its hands well past midnight, leaving less than twenty-four hours to the New Year, he wondered what time and day it was on Guadalcanal.

Resuming typing, he wrote:

As Fate would have it, that small island in the Pacific has become forever entwined with the history of our town, for there one of our young men, John Groover, U.S. Marine Corps, distinguished himself and honored Robinsville and its people with courageous actions in three battles in which he was wounded. After the first two injuries, Johnny returned to his unit to fight again. In another fight in which he received a third wound, he took over a machine gun and killed 200 attacking Japs. Now the Navy Department has wisely taken him out of action in order to bring him back to the United States to serve his country in a different, but no less important, way. When doctors at a Navy hospital in San Francisco give the word, Johnny will join a national tour by movie stars to sell War Bonds.

But first, thanks to a commentary by Alexander Whiteside on his popular radio program "Voice of the People," Johnny Groover will enjoy a furlough in Robinsville, during which he will receive the plaudits of the town.

Typing halted as Scrappy remembered the first time he'd met Aleck Whiteside. They'd both been assigned by competing New York City newspapers to cover the kidnaping of the Lindbergh baby and subsequent trial of the man accused of it. Aleck had scooped his journalistic competitors by getting a jailhouse interview with Bruno Richard Hauptmann on the night of the day he'd been arrested. Whiteside had parlayed that coup and his brilliant reporting of the trial into a radio show of Broadway and Hollywood gossip, political commentary, and a story about a famous crime. The program's most popular feature, it had resulted in Whiteside being awarded a certificate making him an honorary G-Man, presented by FBI Director J. Edgar Hoover.

Still reminiscing, Scrappy remembered the fright in Johnny Groover's blue eyes as his father stood before Judge Albert Wooten and tearfully pleaded to the magistrate not to send his son to prison. No, Johnny hadn't always been the best boy in school, said Harry Groover, taking a day off from his job as a milkman. Johnny wasn't really a bad kid, he said. He'd fallen in with the wrong crowd. The boys who deserved to go to jail were the ones who'd forced Johnny to go along on the armored car stickup. Salvatore Perillo had been the mastermind. Dom always did what his brother told him to do. The Slattery boy had brought a gun that belonged to his older brother. Johnny was just a lookout, along with the youngest Perillo, fifteen-year-old Enrico.

Twenty-year-old Salvatore had gotten the idea because he'd once worked for the armored car firm. Dom was a junior high school dropout with a record of petty thefts. Slattery was an all-around-town ne'er-do-well. All three had been suspected of belonging to a burglary gang that had plagued Bridge Street and other downtown merchants in the months just before the war. In the armored car holdup, they'd gotten away with fifty thousand dollars, none of which was found after they were arrested. Salvatore and Dom had each been sentenced to five years. Pete Slattery had disappeared. His brother Michael said he had no idea where he'd gone and promptly left town, raising suspicions that he'd done so to join Pete on the lam.

On the pleading of the widowed Mrs. Perillo, young Enrico had been sent to the Blessed Heart Boys Reformatory in Norristown.

Thanks to Harry Groover's plea, Johnny had gotten a choice: prison or enlistment in the Marine Corps. Now Johnny was a thrice-wounded war hero, and thanks to a radio commentary made by a friend of both Scrappy Mac-Farland and President Roosevelt, he was to be honored by the nation, starting with his hometown and a rally at Washington Field, to be presided over by Alexander Whiteside himself.

Smiling at the ironies, Scrappy typed:

> Mayor Cantrell has announced that the welcome home for Sgt. Groover will be planned by a committee headed by Mrs. Beatrice Bradshaw and Miss Kate Fallon, organizers of last February's successful V-for-Victory Rally and Dance.

Stirring from these reminiscences, he surveyed the soggy state of his cigar. Judging it to be finished, he placed it in an ashtray to finish the story by bringing it back to its starting point.

> And so, on this New Year's Eve as we bid adieu with satisfaction to a year of promising beginnings, we look forward not only to honoring a hometown hero, but to continued heartening news from the far-flung fields of battle and, with God's grace, a swift conclusion to the war so that we may soon welcome

home all those who serve and whom we love and miss so terribly.

Fifteen minutes later as he lit another La Primadora and looked forward to a reunion with his old friend Aleck Whiteside, the story had been set in type and was rolling off the press in the basement with a satisfying rumble.

3

"**W**HAT A DISGRACE," exclaimed Chief of Police Thomas Detwiler at half past seven as he carried the paper to the kitchen to read with breakfast.

Standing at a counter with her back to him, his plump, jolly wife wiped her hands on her apron and replied, "What's a disgrace, my dear?"

"Not what. Who."

"Very well," she said, opening the sides of the toaster to turn two slices of bread to do the other sides, "who's a disgrace?"

"Our half-witted mayor," said Detwiler, sitting at the table and stabbing the front page of the newspaper with a thick finger, "that's who."

"What's he done now?"

Detwiler picked up the newspaper and waved it. "He is actually going ahead with a big ceremony for the Groover kid. He's probably also planning to give the little crook the damn key to the town."

Mrs. Detwiler half turned to face him. "The boy *is* a war hero."

"He's also a thief."

"That robbery was almost two years ago, Tom," she said, shaking her head. "Let it go."

"I'll let it go," he said, slamming down the paper, "when I find out where those hoodlums hid all that loot so I can turn it over to the owners of the steel plant."

"I believe the loss was covered by insurance, so you'd actually have to turn it over to the insurance company, wouldn't you?"

Glaring at her, Detwiler muttered, "That . . . is . . . not . . . the point."

"Anyway, I don't see what any of this has to do with the mayor having a ceremony for the Groover boy," said Mrs. Detwiler, checking on the toast. "That was then, this is now. The young man is being recognized for what he did in the war. Besides, if Johnny Groover was all that bad, Judge Wooten would have put him in prison with the others."

"That just proves that Mayor Cantrell is not the only nitwit we have in this town. As sure as God made little green apples, Johnny Groover knows where the Slattery kid is, and therefore he knows where the money went."

"Be that as it may," said his wife, removing the toast, "I heard from Beatrice Bradshaw, that President Roosevelt might have the Groover boy at the White House so he can present him with the Congressional Medal of Honor."

"Medal or no medal, he's a crook."

She carried the toast to the table. "The president's a crook?"

"Not him," said Detwiler, slathering the toast with butter. "Johnny Groover!"

"Go easy with that butter, Tom. Mr. Fulmer at the A&P store says there's a shortage. No way of telling when I'll be able to buy more."

"Do you know what this ceremony of the mayor's means? It means that my officers, the very ones who arrested Groover for taking part in that stickup, are going to be *guarding* him."

Thinking back to the day of the arrest, Detwiler vividly recalled taking two men out to Washington Field and finding Johnny Groover in the office of the football coach, Ralph Franklin, calmly waiting to be arrested.

Detwiler's reverie was shattered by his wife's voice. "Well, here's what I think," she said, crossing her arms over her ample bosom. "I think that if Johnny Groover knew where the money from the robbery was hidden, he'd have told you."

Detwiler grunted. "Excuse me, my dear, but you don't know what the hell you're talking about. I questioned that kid for six straight hours. I told him that if he cooperated, I'd put in a good word for him with the judge. He was hard as nails. He practically spit in my face. He's the type that if you beat him with a rubber hose, you couldn't get anything out of him."

"Do you really have a rubber hose at headquarters?"

"Of course not. You know what I mean."

"The boy was that fearless, huh?"

"Like I said, hard as nails."

She smiled, reached out, and tenderly patted his shoulder. "That's what the Japs found out on Guadalcanal. It's why FDR will be giving him the Congressional Medal of Honor."

The long silence that followed was broken only by the sound of the chief of police's teeth biting crisp toast.

4

As Chief Detwiler ate breakfast, in the North Side home of the widow Mrs. Josephine Perillo, the new assistant to Monsignor Giuseppi Federico of St. Ann's was seated in her small, square kitchen.

In the middle of a row of attached wooden two-story homes with porchless fronts, the house seemed to teeter atop a steep-sided ridge that ran like a spine along the north side of Indian Creek, dividing Robinsville almost in half. At its foot sprawled the town's main employer, the Robinsville Steel Company. Through the only window in Mrs. Perillo's kitchen Father Robert Brennan could see thick black smoke rising in straight columns from the mouths of seven tall, slender chimneys of the plant's open hearths.

Freshly graduated from St. Joseph's Seminary in Philadelphia, he had been summoned by Mrs. Perillo's next-door neighbor.

"Josephine won't stop crying," Mrs. Downey had reported. "She's upset on account of what she read in the *Independence* about the town's plan to honor Johnny Groover."

Looking puzzled, the priest had asked, "Why should that upset her?"

"Of course, you're new in town," said Mrs. Downey, "so you wouldn't know about the big payroll robbery at the steel plant the year before last. Josephine's three sons were involved in it, you see. So was Johnny Groover. The Perillo boys got sent up for it, two of them to prison and the youngest, Rico, to the reformatory. His time is just about up, though. I think he's supposed to get out soon. Anyway, Josephine blames Johnny Groover for them being locked up. She thinks he made a deal to save his own neck by turning her boys in to the police. But I know that's not what happened. They were caught because of their big mouths. They couldn't keep their yaps shut about how smart they were. Somebody else turned them in."

"How do you know this?"

"I have a friend on the police force. He said it wasn't the Groover boy who squealed. I've told that to Josephine time and again, but she won't listen."

When the priest followed her into Mrs. Perillo's kitchen, Josephine had looked at him in alarm and demanded, "What are you doing here?"

Looking much too young to be wearing the cassock and collar of the Church, he was tall and rangy with a handsome Gregory Peck face and curly black hair tumbling down his forehead. A long upturned nose reminded her of Bob Hope's.

Slender fingers toyed with a gold chain and crucifix as

he replied, "Mrs. Downey thought I could be of comfort to you."

Clutching the rumpled newspaper, Josephine sobbed, "It's not fair that my three boys are locked up and the Groover kid got off. And now he gets treated like all of a sudden he's some kind of saint. It's not right. How could God let this happen? I pray every day for my boys to come home. I light candles. I say the rosary. I'm at mass three times a week! But my beautiful boys are still locked up and Johnny Groover is now a big hero. I wish he was coming home in a pine box."

Father Brennan glanced anxiously at Mrs. Downey, took a deep breath, and softly said to Josephine, "No you don't. You really can't wish that."

"It may be a sin to say it," she cried, "but as God is my witness, I won't be happy until that rotten kid is six feet under."

"I think what we should do," said the priest, taking her hands between his, "is pray that God will grant that your sons come home soon. I think we should also pray for the Groover boy."

Josephine jerked away her hands. "It's lucky for him that my husband is dead and gone, because if Vittoro were here when that boy comes home, he would take the revolver that he keeps in the bureau drawer and send that kid's soul where it belongs, burning in Hell. So there's no use wasting your time talking to me about prayer, Father. I don't mean to be disrespectful, but I don't want you here." Her eyes turned toward Mrs. Downey. "And you neither, Molly."

Mrs. Downey's eyes welled with tears. "I was only trying to help."

"Just leave me alone. Both of you."

As they stepped from the house, the priest let out a long sigh and patted Mrs. Downey on the shoulder. "Try not to feel upset or angry, Mrs. Downey," he said. "You did the right thing."

Walking back to the church, he noticed that wind was blowing from the north, dispelling the seven black plumes of the steel plant's smokestacks and spreading them over the south side of town like a low overcast.

5

A FEW MINUTES BEFORE eight o'clock, Ralph Franklin
was beginning the last phase of his morning two-mile
run by turning the corner of Jessup and Hoover Streets. In
the middle of the block stood the modest brick house that
had been his home for nearly ten years, since he had been
hired to coach Robinsville High's Phantoms football
team. The assignment also included being the gym teacher
and lecturing junior and senior boys once a week on hygiene and health, though *not,* principal Felix Dobson
warned, on the how-to's of human sexual intercourse.

Nearing his house, Ralph saw that the newspaper delivery boy's pitch had failed to fling the *Independence* onto
the porch. The tightly folded paper had fallen short by ten
feet and landed in the driveway between the right front
wheel of his Ford coupe and a clump of grayish ice, the
only remnant of last week's two-inch snowfall. Loping
across the lawn, he dipped into a slight crouch without

breaking stride, scooped up the paper, and bounded onto the porch. Pausing to let his breathing subside to normal, he read the main headline and smiled.

Going into the house, he had no difficulty picturing Johnny Groover muscling his way through the jungles of Guadalcanal. The star he'd coached in football would go at the Japanese as fearlessly as he'd scampered through holes in the line that had been cleared by Richie Zale, then dodged tacklers on the Washington Field gridiron. Trophies symbolic of the combined talents of Groover and Zale, which had given Robinsville its three conference championships, stood in a display case in the coach's office. In a locker were Johnny's muddy white jersey with the big purple 7 and the uniform with number 11 that Richie Zale had worn during their final game. Along with these was a brown paper-wrapped package that he was keeping until Johnny returned from the war.

Accepting Johnny Groover as a war hero was not difficult. But the image of him that formed as the coach climbed the stairs to take a shower and dress for school was of a scared, bewildered fifteen-year-old boy seated in the office next to the locker room.

"You remember what you said when I first tried out for the football team and you said you were going to put me in the starting lineup," Johnny had said that afternoon, "and you told me that if there was ever anything I needed to talk about, but didn't know who to talk to, that I could always come to you and what I said would be kept between the two of us?"

"That's what I said then and it still goes. So, what is it you want to talk about?"

"It's kind of embarrassing."

"That's okay. Just come out with it."

"It's about, uh, when a guy is with a girl, and they've been necking, and uh, she says she's willing to let him go all the way. But she tells him he has to have, uh, protection, or she won't."

"My advice, Johnny, is that you don't do it. I mean, don't go all the way with the girl. You and she are too young for that."

"Yeah, well, you see, we've already . . ."

"Done it?"

"Yeah. I got what she said I had to use. My old man had some in his dresser drawer."

"Okay. You and the girl did it and you used a rubber. I can't say I approve of what you did, but since you did, it was smart of you to have protection."

"The thing I have to ask you is whether it's possible that even if a guy used a rubber that the girl could still get, uh, knocked up?"

"When did you and the girl have intercourse?"

"Last Saturday night. My folks went out to the movies, and Millie, uh, the *girl* and me, we were supposed to go on a date, but we went to my house instead. If it turns out she is knocked up, I'll be a dead man."

"I know Millie's father. He won't kill you, but he will probably insist that you become his son-in-law."

"How can I get married? I'm only fifteen."

Luckily for Johnny and Mildred Parker, there had been no pregnancy until after Millie had graduated from high school and surprised everyone by marrying Richard Zale. Declared 4-F in the draft because of a back injury he'd gotten playing football, Richie was assistant foreman in the rolling mill at the steel plant. Their son Donald was now almost two. Elizabeth, their daughter, was six months old.

Had Johnny Groover gotten Millie pregnant, Coach Franklin mused as he got into the shower, he might have become a steel worker instead of a kid who had gotten into trouble with the law and wound up in the Marines. And Robinsville would not be preparing to hail him as a certified hero.

6

ABOUT HALF A mile north of Ralph Franklin's residence, at exactly eight o'clock, a whistle on the roof of the rolling mill signaled the end of the overnight shift. As the final shriek of the whistle echoed off the North Side bluff, the foreman, Mike O'Donnell, as ardent a Phantoms fan as the team had ever had, fell into step beside his assistant. "So, Richie," he said, "you must be pretty excited that you'll be seeing your old teammate again, huh?"

Ruggedly handsome with cornsilk hair and piercing eyes, Richard Zale had used his powerful torso and strong legs during four winning Phantoms football seasons to open up defensive lines so quarterback Johnny Groover could prance through almost untouched. Then came the last game of their final year, when Richie had to be carried off the field with an injured back in the third quarter.

"Johnny Groover a war hero!" said Mike. "Forgetting

about the trouble that he got into because he fell in with the wrong crowd, I always knew that boy had the right stuff and would turn out all right. I guess the two of you will be having a big reunion."

"I'd sure like to, Mike," said Richie as they left the mill to walk to their cars, "but I'm not sure how much time Johnny will have to spare. His dad says the government's got him lined up for a lot of traveling. He's going on tour to sell war bonds."

"Maybe so, but I can't imagine him not finding some time to see you again. What a pair the two of you made. Saturday afternoons at Washington Field haven't been the same in the two years since you boys graduated."

"Well, like the man says at the end of *The March of Time* newsreel at the movies," said Richie as he got into his car, "time marches on."

"You're right about that. Here we are about to ring in a new year, but it seems like it was yesterday that the Japs bombed Pearl Harbor. Let's hope 1943's as good a year for us in the war that this one's been. Tell that great wife of yours that I wish her a Happy New Year."

The sound of the steel mill's whistle had alerted Mildred Zale that she had fifteen minutes until Richie came in the front door expecting to find his breakfast of ham, two sunny-side-up eggs, fried potatoes, four pieces of toast, and black coffee on the kitchen table. Only after he'd eaten would he go into the kids' bedroom to see how they were, peeking in on the way to the bathroom to take a shower. When that was done, he expected her to be back in bed as he entered the bedroom naked and ready, with bath water beaded on the broad, muscular shoulders that had made him a star blocker. But five minutes after getting into bed, he would roll off her and fall asleep. A moment later she would go quietly downstairs and back to the kitchen to clear the table and wash the dishes, pots, and pans.

Also expected to be on the kitchen table when Richie came home was the *Independence*.

When he picked it up this morning, he looked at the front page and grinned.

"Leave it to Johnny," he said, lifting his coffee cup as if it were a cocktail and he was making a toast. "If there's a way to get out of a tight spot, that boy will find it, even if it means getting out of the Marines by being shot by a couple of Japs."

Millie frowned. "I don't think Johnny went in the Marines intending to get wounded."

"I wouldn't be surprised if good old Johnny pumped the bullets into his arm, leg, and chest by himself."

She sat opposite him with a cup of coffee. "That's ridiculous. Why on earth would he do such a thing?"

"To earn a one-way ticket home, of course."

"You forget that he joined the Marines to get out of this town."

"But now he's coming home a hero, all is forgiven. I'll bet right now, wherever Johnny is, he's licking his chops over the idea that some night while I'm working my ass off at the plant, he'll sneak in here so you and him can spend eight hours going at it, like the two of you used to when we were in school."

She jerked with shock, spilling her coffee.

"Don't try to deny it, Millie," he said. "Everybody in

high school knew what was going on between you two, and had been going on since the tenth grade."

She bolted up. "Well, everybody was wrong."

"Come on, admit it."

"If you believed that," she said with fists against her hips, "why did you marry me?"

The smile disappeared. "Because I had to. Or *thought* I had to."

Her fists uncurled as her arms fell to her sides. "What the devil does that mean?"

He lurched up from the table. "You know damn well."

She gasped. "Are you insinuating that Donnie isn't your son?"

He strode toward the door. "I'm *saying* it."

Pursuing him, she yelled, "Oh really? Then whose son is he?"

He turned around angrily. "Well, he sure doesn't look like me, does he? You don't have to be Sherlock Holmes to see that he's the spitting image of Johnny Groover."

Fists again on hips, she laughed. "I see! You believe Johnny Groover got me pregnant, and I tricked you into thinking it was you who did it."

Standing in the doorway, he replied, "That's exactly what happened. You knew that you could never get him to marry you because he was going to be locked up in prison for that payroll robbery. But big surprise! He didn't go to jail. He went into the Marines. Only by that time you'd convinced me it was our kid you were pregnant with, so I wound up *having* to marry you."

"It's not true. Not a bit of it. And I can prove it."

"Really? How?"

"Johnny Groover was your best friend. You were so

close the kids at school called you the Dynamic Duo, like Batman and Robin in the comic books. On and off the football field he was Batman and you were his Boy Wonder. If I had been screwing Johnny, you would have known because he would have told his Robin. If you had known Johnny and I were lovers, you wouldn't have married me."

"You got that part right," he said, leaning against the door jamb, "but you're wrong that Johnny would have told me. He wasn't the kind of guy who would screw a girl and then brag of it to buddies, including me. Johnny may be a crook and all-around sharp operator at working the angles, but he's a gentleman. Johnny never squeals."

"Since he's such a gentleman," she said, standing close enough to kiss him, "and since you think Donnie is Johnny's kid, how come Johnny never offered to marry me?"

"He didn't know you were pregnant. You didn't tell him because there was no way you were going to be married to a guy who was about to be sent to prison. As for me, I was a sap . . . a dreamy-eyed, gullible sap who was madly in love with you. You knew that, and you saw a way out of a spot by telling me that the bun in your oven was mine. You couldn't have Batman, so you settled for Robin instead."

He came up straight and stepped into a small hallway. Looking back at her, he stopped halfway up the stairs to the second floor.

"There's nothing we can do about it now," he continued. "We're Catholic, so divorce is out of the question. Besides, I know Elizabeth is my daughter, so let's just drop the subject, all right? I'm going to look in on the kids and take a bath, so you get yourself upstairs and into the bedroom. I'm feeling horny as hell this morning."

"I think the reason you're horny," she shouted as he started up the stairs, "is that you're looking forward to Batman and Robin being together again."

With reddening face, he whirled around. "Just what the hell are you driving at?"

She smiled slyly. "The kids in school always said you and Johnny were queer for each other, always playing grab ass in the showers after gym class and in the field house locker room after games. I didn't believe it then. But now I wonder."

Down the steps in an instant, he slapped her face so hard that as she stumbled backward she thought he'd punched her.

Rubbing her stinging cheek as he bounded up the steps, she yelled, "That's the reason you're feeling hot and bothered. Johnny's coming home."

When the bathroom door slammed, the bang started Elizabeth crying in the next room. A moment later, Donnie was also awake and yelling, "Mommy! Mommy! I'm scared."

Going into the tiny bedroom, she lifted the brown-haired, brown-eyed boy from his bed. "It's all right, my darling. There's nothing to be scared of. Mommy's here."

7

NANCY ROBERTS ENTERED her older sister's bedroom carrying the *Independence* opened before her like a shield so that Patricia would notice the photo of Johnny Groover on the front page. Seated at a vanity table brushing long red hair, Pat saw it in the mirror.

"Now that your old boyfriend is coming home a hero," Nancy said, settling onto Pat's bed, "are you sorry that you sent him that letter breaking up with him? They call that a Dear John letter. In this case it really was."

"Why should I be sorry?" said Pat, going to the bed and grabbing the paper. Studying the picture, she continued, "Johnny being a war hero doesn't change anything between us. He's a big boy. He'll understand that I'm not in love with him anymore."

She put down the paper and returned to the vanity.

"I'm not sure I ever was in love with him," she said, checking her makeup. "Or if he was in love with me."

"Really? You certainly made a convincing show of it. Johnny spent more nights in our house than he did in his own. Are you going to see him when he comes home?"

Satisfied with her rouge and lipstick, Pat turned to face her sister. "I doubt very much that he'll be interested in seeing me again."

Nancy lay on her side, looking at the photograph and stroking it with a fingertip. "He's been away a long time. He might be so hungry for a girl that he's willing to forget that he ever got that letter."

"I'm sure that if he's hungry for a girl," said Pat, opening a closet to take out the dress she had chosen to wear to her job as a teller at the Farmer's and Mechanics National Bank, "that he'll take care of his need well before he gets off the train at the Reading Station. Knowing him, I'd say that by now he's hooked up with several."

Nancy sat up. "Did you ever consider that he might not have received your letter?"

"He must have gotten it," Pat said, slipping into an emerald green frock. "I haven't heard from him since I sent it."

Nancy frowned. "He was fighting in some jungle somewhere. He might not have been able to write to you."

Buttoning the high collar of the dress, Pat replied, "He's been in hospitals in Hawaii and on the West Coast for a couple of months, where I'm sure he would have been able to write me a letter if he wanted to. Besides which, I told him in the letter that I've found someone else."

Nancy looked again at the photograph in the paper. "I wonder if he got the letter before or after he was wounded. Maybe he got it before and was so crushed by reading what you said that he wasn't paying attention to the war, and that's why he got shot."

Pat shut the closet door forcefully. "For gosh sakes, Nan, will you please stop going on about the letter? It's not as if I'm the first girl to break off a relationship with Johnny Groover. There were three before me that I know of, and that was just in high school. Who knows how many girls he might have gone out with before that?"

"He sure was a dreamboat," said Nancy, smiling. "I hope being through the war hasn't changed his looks. Since you're not interested in him anymore, maybe I'll see if he'll go out with me. He's always had a romantic aura of danger around him, kind of like John Garfield in *Dust Be My Destiny* and *Castle on the Hudson*." She paused and thought a moment. "I wonder why you always see John Garfield in movies where he's in prison? I like dangerousness in guys."

"Nancy Roberts," said Pat, sitting on the bed to put on sensible, black, low-heeled shoes, "you are a scandal in the making."

"Have you got a date tonight with your new love from the Army hospital—Corporal, uh, what's his name?"

Pat stood. "Bobby Gordon."

"Is he tall, dark, and handsome?"

"I wouldn't say he's handsome," Pat said, going to the vanity to pick up her purse. "He's more like . . . cute."

"Where's he from?"

"Boston. He's got this funny way of talking. He says things like 'caah' for car and 'yaad' for yard. He calls a milkshake a frap."

"What does he do at the hospital?"

"He's in the military police and pulls sentry duty on the main gate."

"Pulls?"

"It's an Army word. You pull sentry duty. You pull KP, which means—"

"Kitchen police. Peeling potatoes and stuff. I saw Abbott and Costello in *Buck Privates* and Jimmy Durante in *You're in the Army Now.* How old is Bobby?"

"Twenty-five."

"*Twenty-five?* Wow, that's old."

"For someone seventeen such as you, it's old. I being almost twenty, it's just right."

"Are you going to let him go all the way?"

"Nancy! Please! Go to school. You'll be late."

"What time is Bobby picking you up tonight?"

"He isn't. We're going to the seven o'clock movie at the Colonial. Bobby gets off duty at six-thirty, so he's meeting me there."

Nancy rose from the bed and sauntered toward the door. Looking back at Pat, she said in a teasing tone, "Seats in the last row of the balcony so you can neck, of course."

8

THE LAST *INDEPENDENCE* that ten-year-old Jimmy Trainer had to deliver on his route would not be plucked from the big wooden mail box at Mr. Turner's ramshackle dwelling on the far end of Baxter Lane until the middle of the afternoon. This was because sixty-year-old Delmer Turner went right to bed as soon as he got home from his job. Employed as weeknight watchman in the Graf & Son Movers and Fireproof Storage Co., he had been working from ten o'clock in the evening until six in the morning, Sunday through Thursday, for a little more than a year.

He'd been hired by Gerald Graf, who'd explained that his primary duty was to look out for fires, but he and Delmer understood his being hired and the job itself were a charade. The company that advertised its fireproof warehouse had not had one fire in its hundred-year history. The job offer had been a friendly gesture by Gerald for an unfortunate friend of his father who'd been unable to find work for more than a year.

Unwisely, but understandably, Delmer had let his good nature and humanity get in the way of the vigilance expected of an employee of the Swift-as-Mercury Messenger Service. On a Friday morning in late August 1941, Delmer was driving a small armored van on Coldstream Road. As the truck passed a densely wooded area and through a kind of tunnel formed by the overhanging branches of trees, in the back of the truck were several canvas bags containing fifty thousand dollars for the payroll of the Robinsville Steel Company.

As Delmer looked ahead, he saw what appeared to be an injured boy. He lay on his back beside a smashed-up-looking bicycle in the middle of the road. Delmer assumed that the lad must have been hit by a car while on his way to a swimming hole created by a makeshift dam across Indian Creek, which boys had maintained for decades.

Stopping the van, he bounded out to see whether the motionless boy was alive.

Bending over the twisted figure and noting that the boy was breathing, Delmer was astonished to see that the boy's face was masked by a Boy Scout's neckerchief.

Then he heard noises behind him that sounded like someone pushing through roadside underbrush. A moment later, he heard, "Okay, old man, don't make a move. We want all the money."

The voice sounded young.

Turning slightly, Delmer found himself facing two figures wearing black masks like the one worn by the Lone Ranger.

He also saw that the taller of them held a pistol. Waving it toward the truck, he demanded, "Don't try to be funny and go for your gun, old man. Just open up the truck and hand over the dough."

By now the boy with the Boy Scout neckerchief was on his feet. Giggling as he yanked Delmer's gun from its holster and flung it toward the woods, he said, "Wow, the jerk really fell for that corny trick."

With his pistol retrieved and the three boys gone, having dashed into the woods with the money bags, Delmer sped in the van toward Robinsville to report the robbery to the police. As he related the story to Chief of Police Detwiler, he was not sure what had been more humiliating to him, falling for the ruse, or being called an old man and a jerk.

"There were three of them?" asked Detwiler.

"Yes," said Delmer. "Three boys. The one with the bicycle and two who came out of the woods when I was trying to help the one in the road."

Looking at another policeman, Officer Todd Doebling, the chief said, "Ten-to-one it's the Perillo boys. Take Dicky Davis with you to the North Side and see if they're home."

As Sherman started to leave, he asked Delmer, "Did I hear right? The kid that was in the road took your gun away from you?"

Too embarrassed to speak, Delmer answered with a nod.

"Did the kid have gloves on?"

"Gloves? No, I don't think so."

"He took it from your holster by grabbing it by the grip?"

"Yes. He yanked it out and threw it in the woods."

"Good," said Davis. "Keep the gun in the holster and leave them both with us. I just hope the kid who handled it left fingerprints."

Unfortunately, when Doebling and Davis went to the Perillo home, the boys' mother gave them an alibi. "My boys couldn'ta robbed nobody," she said indignantly. "They were all here at home. My boys are good boys."

That evening Chief Detwiler had received an anonymous phone call in which a fourth name was mentioned: Johnny Groover. But after six hours of questioning in which he confessed to taking part in the robbery, he steadfastly refused to implicate the Perillos.

The break had come when a thumbprint from the grip of Delmer's gun matched one of Enrico Perillo's prints in the files. Informed of this, the boy broke into tears and confessed that he, his brothers, and Pete Slattery had pulled the robbery while Johnny Groover had acted as the lookout. Johnny was arrested the next day. But when the police went to pick up Slattery, they'd found that he'd skipped town, evidently taking the loot with him.

A week after the Perillos and Johnny Groover were arrested, Delmer was summoned to the office of the president of Swift-as-Mercury Messenger Company in Pottstown and fired. His numerous attempts to find employment in the next year had proved unavailing, until Gerald Graf decided that he would sleep better knowing that someone would be wide awake to assure that his storage warehouse didn't suddenly catch fire and burn down.

Because Salvatore, Dominic, and Enrico Perillo had pleaded guilty, and Johnny Groover got a break from the judge, there had been no need for Delmer to go through the humiliation of testifying on that Friday morning in 1941 he had been a first-class jerk.

He had hoped that foolish boys who'd caused his humiliation by taking advantage of his good nature would apologize to him for the misery they'd caused him.

None had.

9

A FEW MINUTES AFTER five o'clock on the production line of Manyon's Precision Metal Company, Kate Fallon finished the last spot-weld of a nine-hour shift. She switched off the torch and hung it on a hook, then removed her welder's mask and laid it on the workbench. Wiping beads of sweat from her forehead with the back of a hand, she turned to Grace Fulmer and said, "Another day, another dollar."

Undoing a yellow bandanna, she freed bobbed brown hair and looked forward to a hot bath and her mother's usual Wednesday night supper of dried beef in a thick white gravy served over mashed potatoes.

As she and Grace headed from the welding shop to the locker room that Mr. Manyon had created to accommodate the half-a-dozen women whom he had hired during the war, Grace asked, "What are you doing tonight to ring out the old and ring in the new?"

Three years behind Kate in school, Grace had been head cheerleader and voted by senior classmates as "most beautiful." Although they had believed she was head-over-heels in love with the class clown, Johnny Groover, right after graduation she'd surprised everyone by marrying the handsome captain of the football team and class president, Jimmy Hollander. Now Jimmy was in the Army somewhere, Grace was doing her bit in the war effort on the homefront by working as a welder, and Johnny was recuperating in San Francisco from wounds he'd gotten at Guadalcanal and would soon return home as a certified hero.

"No matter how tired I might feel," Kate replied to Grace's question as they got out of the gray coveralls they wore for work, "I will force myself to stay up long enough to listen to Guy Lombardo and His Royal Canadians play 'Auld Lang Syne.'"

"I'd do the same thing," said Grace, "but I'm sure that if I did, I'd break down and cry." She shrugged and smiled. "I probably will anyway. It's the first New Year's Eve that Jimmy and I aren't together since we got married."

Putting on a gray overcoat with fox fur collar, Kate thought about her fiancé. "This is my second without Mike."

As they left the locker room, Grace asked, "How is he? Do you know where he is?"

"The last I heard from him, he was in England," Kate said. "Of course, he couldn't come right out and say so in his letter. But he dropped a few clues. Since I haven't heard from him in a while, and since he's on Eisenhower's staff, I assume he's somewhere in North Africa."

Grace's eyes brimmed with tears. "I think that's where Jimmy might be. Maybe him and Mike will run into one another. Wouldn't that be something? I can just imagine the two of them carousing in some bar together, can't you?"

"Mike was never much for carousing. But who knows? There *is* a war on, as they say."

The tears in Grace's eyes subsided. With forced cheeriness, she asked, "Did you see that new movie with Humphrey Bogart and Ingrid Bergman?"

Kate turned up the coat collar in preparation for going out into the cold. "*Casablanca?* Yes. I took my brother Paulie to see it. Of course, being eight years old, he was disappointed that it was a love story. Once Peter Lorre was arrested, Paulie lost interest. It was a good picture."

"Maybe Jimmy and Mike will meet in some place like Rick's, the club in the movie."

"Well, if they do," said Kate as they left the factory to join a group of men waiting at a bus stop, "I hope there's no woman there who's as beautiful as Ingrid Bergman."

"If you had been Ilsa," Grace asked as a bus made a turn from the road into a curving driveway in front of Manyon's to pick up the plant's workers, "could you have left Rick and gone away with Victor?"

"Ilsa *was* Victor's wife, Grace."

"That didn't keep her from having an affair with Rick in Paris."

"When they were lovers in Paris," said Kate as the bus stopped and the door opened, "Ilsa believed Victor was dead."

"Paul Henreid is *so* handsome," said Grace as the men waited and let the women board the bus first. "I loved him in *Now Voyager.* When he lit two cigarettes at once and gave one to Bette Davis, I thought I'd just die, it was so romantic. But I guess things like that happen only in movies, right? I mean, did Mike ever light two cigarettes at once and hand you one?"

"No, but not because he's unromantic," said Kate, sitting by a window as Grace sat next to her. "He prefers a pipe, and I'm not a smoker."

"Jimmy smokes like a chimney," said Grace as the bus began moving. "I used to yell at him about cigarettes all the time. Now I'd give anything to see him lighting one up."

"I know what you mean. I miss the aroma of Mike's pipe tobacco. So here we are, a pair of spoken-for ladies with nothing to do on New Year's Eve but sit in front of the radio and listen to Guy Lombardo's orchestra. We're like the song. 'Don't Get Around Much Anymore.'"

Nothing more was said until the bus halted at Grace's stop. Leaving Kate, she smiled and said, "Happy New Year to you and your folks."

Ten minutes later, Kate left the bus on the corner opposite the West End firehouse, where Mike had been a volunteer. Every place in town, it seemed, was a reminder of him. Yet now and then she found herself unable to remember his face or to recall the sound of his voice. At other times, such as when Mr. Manyon was smoking his pipe, or when she heard a burst of laughter from one of the men on the welding line, she could see him as clearly as a closeup in a movie. A song on the radio or a jukebox could do the same.

Walking three blocks from her bus stop to her house, she found herself humming "Don't Get Around Much

Anymore" and knew that for the rest of the night she would not be able to get it out of her head, just as she'd been unable to forget "As Time Goes By" for three days after she'd seen *Casablanca*. Entering the large house with white clapboard siding, a huge front porch, and green-trimmed windows that her grandfather had built at the turn of the century, she paused to breathe in the aroma of stuffed cabbage.

Her mother shouted from the kitchen, "Is that you, Kate?"

"Yes, and I've brought Eleanor Roosevelt home to dinner," she replied, taking off her coat. "Is that okay?"

She looked into the parlor. Her brother Paulie sprawled on his belly in the middle of the room, facing the big Atwater-Kent radio and listening to "Jack Armstrong, All-American Boy." Going into the room, she nudged his ribs with a toe. "Hey, boy, shouldn't you be in your room doing your homework?"

Paulie made a face. "Don't have any."

"Well, you ought to."

As Kate went into the kitchen and found her mother at the stove, Mrs. Fallon announced, "Beatrice Bradshaw phoned a few minutes ago. She wants you to call her. She said she'll be at her bookstore doing inventory until nine o'clock."

"Working on New Year's Eve," said Kate as she turned to go back to the parlor, where the phone was kept. "That's typical of her."

Paulie's program was offering a commercial for Wheaties as Kate's call was answered on the first ring. "This is The Book Nook. Good evening. Mrs. Bradshaw speaking."

"Hello, Mrs. Bee, it's Kate."

"My dear, we've got to have a meeting as soon as possible. Mayor Cantrell heard from someone in Washington, the Navy or the Treasury Department, I'm not sure which, about the government's plans regarding the furlough for the Groover boy. Evidently, we are to expect him in Robinsville on the *twelfth*."

"Gosh, that's a week earlier than we were told to expect him."

"Mayor Cantrell wants to see our proposed program as soon as possible. Can you and I meet about it at my house at one o'clock on Sunday?"

"Of course."

"Mr. MacFarland will also be there. By the way, did you see today's paper?"

"Not yet. It's delivered after I go to work."

"It's got a very nice story by Mr. MacFarland which mentions that we are arranging the festivities for the Groover boy. Now I'm sure you've got plans for this evening, so I'll just wish you and your family a Happy New Year."

"The same to you, Mrs. Bee."

As Kate put down the phone, Paulie blurted out, "Your name was in the newspaper again."

"I know. What did it say about me?"

Paulie shrugged. "Dunno, I didn't read it. Mom told me it was in there. Ask her."

Returning to the kitchen, Kate said, "I hear my name's in the newspaper."

"Mr. MacFarland wrote about what a good year this has been on account of our victories in the war, and how you and Mrs. Bradshaw are in charge of planning the welcome home party for the Groover boy," said Mrs Fallon. "Who would've thought that smart-aleck kid would end up a war hero?"

As she carried a bowl of steaming mashed potatoes to a table set for three, Kate felt a pang of nostalgia. Before the war, there would have been seven plates, but her father was working overtime at the steel mill, brother Jack was flying a dive-bomber plane in the Navy, her older sister Jean was a nurse in a Naval hospital near Washington, and younger sister Arlene and members of her class were volunteers two evenings a week at the Army hospital.

"Paulie, supper's ready," Mrs. Fallon shouted. "Turn off that darned radio and come and get it before it gets cold."

With supper finished, the dishes washed, and her mother and Paulie in the parlor listening to a quiz show on the radio, Kate took the newspaper up to her bedroom to read what Scrappy MacFarland had written and to write a letter to Mike. Not knowing how long it would be until he read it, or if it would reach him at all, she wrote:

My darling,

As I write this, a new year is only hours away and it seems as if it was only yesterday that you and I were dancing to the "swing and sway" music of Sammy Kaye's orchestra in Philadelphia as we prepared to welcome in 1941. I can hardly believe it was two years ago. Back then I was a happy secretary working at the steel plant and looking forward to you graduating from law school and to the day

*when I would become Mrs. Michael King. Now I'm
a welder at Manyon's, you are an officer in the army
and we have no idea when we'll be together again.
But I know that happy day* will *come, and God willing, it won't be too long in coming.*

I'm enclosing a wonderful article in today's Independence *that Scrappy MacFarland wrote. You'll
read that Mrs. Bee and I have been asked by Mayor
Cantrell to arrange the town's welcome-home ceremony for our local war hero, Johnny Groover. As
I'm sure you can imagine, everyone in town is astonished that one of the boys who took part in robbing the steel company payroll last year turned out
to be a hero in the battle for Guadalcanal. But I
guess war changes people. Anyway, the mayor
wants us to go all out in arranging the salute. We're
to have a meeting on Sunday to discuss the final de-
tails. The mayor wants it to be held at the football
field because it's the only place in town big enough
to hold the large number of people expected to attend, and because Johnny Groover was such a big
football star.*

*You will not be surprised that my father is not at
all happy at the thought of Mayor Cantrell presenting the "key to the city" to one of what he calls "the
gang of five" who pulled the biggest robbery in
Robinsville's history. I know a lot of people in town
agree with Dad that we should not be honoring
Johnny Groover. But it's not as if Johnny was the
one who pulled the gun on Mr. Turner.*

*How would it look if the people in Johnny
Groover's hometown didn't do something to honor*

*him when he'll be going to the White House to re-
ceive the Congressional Medal of Honor from the
President of the United States?*

Pausing in writing, Kate recalled a night, two years ago,
when she had been in Buster's Restaurant after taking
Paulie to see a spy movie, *Saboteur,* starring Robert Cum-
mings, at the Colonial Theater. She had found Johnny
Groover at the soda fountain, flirting with the waitress,
Nancy Edinger. Also in Buster's that night was Sal Perillo.
He'd been giving Nancy such a hard time that she'd
kicked him and his friends out. She had been found murdered the next day. Sal and his two pals had been Chief of
Police Detwiler's prime suspects. But to his dismay and to
the shock of the town, Nancy's murder and a later murder
of a popular Robinsville High School history teacher had
been committed by a member of the police force.

That Johnny Groover had become involved with Sal
Perillo and Sal's two brothers in planning the steel mill
payroll robbery had not come as a surprise to Detwiler,
Kate recalled. But the news had been painful to her, not
only because she had always looked on Johnny as a lik-
able, harmless rogue, but because it had broken the heart
of Johnny's father. When Judge Wooten took pity on Mr.
Groover by offering Johnny a choice between prison and
the Marines, she had been glad for Mr. Groover's sake.

Returning to Mike's letter, she wrote, "Isn't it ironic
that a boy who was voted 'most likely to wind up in
prison' will now be getting the red carpet treatment?"

Pausing once more, she hoped that the people of
Robinsville would forgive, even if they were unable to
forget. As always when a crime occurred, she ruminated,

many more people had been affected by the deed than the driver of the van who'd been held up and the four boys who'd done it. Saddest of all had been the parents of the boys.

According to a regular customer of Mrs. Bee's bookstore and a neighbor of Mrs. Perillo, the devout elderly woman's spirit had been crushed. Embittered because her sons had been put in jails and a reform school while Johnny Groover was spared incarceration, Mrs. Perillo had told her neighbor that if her husband were alive, "Big Sal" would have taken his pistol and gotten his revenge, not just on Johnny, but against the judge who'd let him off.

As to Mr. Groover, although he'd done his best to deal with the humiliation and get on with his work, sympathetic customers on his dairy delivery route could not fail to notice that he was not the same jolly milkman they had known.

Looking at her bedside clock and noting that it would soon be midnight, Kate decided to suspend writing the letter and complete it tomorrow night.

In bed at a few minutes before twelve, she wound her bedside alarm clock, checked that it was set to wake her at six o'clock, and switched on the radio. Tuning it, she found the station that broadcast Guy Lombardo and his orchestra from the ballroom of the Waldorf-Astoria Hotel in New York.

With the little light of the radio dial casting a faint, soft yellow glow in the bedroom, she listened to the Royal Canadians and their "Sweetest music this side of heaven" version of "That Old Black Magic."

When the song ended, their always jovial leader announced in his smoothest tones, "It's half-a-minute to midnight, folks, so all of you out there from coast to coast in the radio audience, please join the ladies and gentleman here at the Waldorf-Astoria in counting down the last ten seconds to the New Year."

At midnight as a cheer went up from the ballroom crowd and the orchestra played "Auld Lang Syne," Lombardo said, "Happy New Year, everybody . . . a very . . . *Happy* . . . New Year."

Longing to salute the moment with Mike, Kate felt tears trickling down her cheeks. She imagined they were his kisses.

10

WHEN THE SINGING of "Auld Lang Syne" ended at Alexander Whiteside's New Year's Eve party, Police Commissioner Valentine asked his host, "So, Aleck, what's the New Year hold for you? Nothing to cause us concern at police headquarters, I hope."

"Getting arrested is not on my schedule," said Aleck with a chuckle, "but one never can know what fate has in store."

Valentine studied Aleck's face intently.

Aleck demanded, "Why are you looking at me as though my face was a mug shot?"

"How's your health? I've been hearing that you've not been feeling so well of late."

Aleck dipped a pudgy hand into a pocket of his crimson smoking jacket and took out a small bottle. "Nitroglycerine tablets," he said, removing the cap. He tapped a thumb to his big chest. "Ticker problems. Nothing to worry about." A small pill went from hand to mouth. "My doctors want to keep me alive. I want to *live*. Therefore, on the nineteenth of January, my fifty-sixth birthday, health be damned and come hell or high water, I intend to celebrate the occasion with a nice luncheon for three of my favorite ladies, Mrs. Roosevelt, Helen Keller, and Madame Chiang Kai-shek."

Valentine let out a little whistle and said admiringly, "That is quite a trio."

Aleck gazed across the room at Harpo Marx offering a solo performance.

"Dear Harpo would call it a trifecta," Aleck said, returning the pill to the pocket. "But in the meantime I shall begin the year 1943 by going to the Paramount Theater tomorrow to take in the stage show featuring the Benny Goodman orchestra and the sensational idol of the bobby sox set, the skinny, bow-tie-wearing, Italian crooner by the name of Frank Sinatra."

Valentine frowned. "I'll be there, too."

"Lew, you surprise me! I had no idea you were a fan of swing music."

"The music is fine, but that's not while I'll be present. The department's been tipped that the publicity people for the Paramount are bringing in hundreds, maybe thousands of teenagers, mostly girls, to put on their own show by screaming and yelling for Frankie."

"How very smart of the boys at Paramount!"

"It's shaping up to be a real mob scene," Valentine continued, "so you might want to rethink your plans. It might not be a good spot to be in for a man with a heart condition."

"Nevertheless, I shall be there. Then I'll be heading off

to a small town in Pennsylvania to be master of ceremonies as the citizens welcome home a local war hero."

"Aleck Whiteside leaving the city and going to a small
town? Does Winchell know this?"

"Perhaps you've read of the young hero in the newspapers. His name is John Groover."

Valentine nodded. "I have. It's said that he practically
beat the Japs on Guadalcanal all by himself. I took the stories with a grain of salt as wartime propaganda."

"When I was staying at the White House just before
Christmas, President Roosevelt told me they're all true.
It's a great example of valor and courage."

"If FDR says it's true, it must be."

"Tell Mayor La Guardia for me that the city should give
this boy a ticker-tape parade—"

"Parades are suspended for the duration."

"Then a City Hall ceremony giving the kid the key to
the city."

"That's a possibility."

"Just as interesting to me in my visit to this small
town," Aleck continued, "is that in the past two years the
place has seen an amazing rise in its rate of crime. I'm
told by an old friend, who's the editor of the town's newspaper, that there have been several murders, an arson fire,
a case of blackmail involving the town's leading women,
and a daring stickup of a payroll delivery truck in which
the young man who's being honored as a hero had been a
participant."

Valentine's eyes went wide. "How the devil did a
stickup man become a war hero? No, don't tell me. I'll tell
you. He managed to persuade a soft-hearted judge to let
him serve his time in the service."

"The Marine Corps. There's another angle to this small-town story that I find irresistible, and that should be fascinating to you, also. As you know, I have made it an avocation of mine to study famous crimes, especially murders. I am *the* authority on the Lizzie Borden case."

"You'll get no argument on that score from me."

"Well, get this, Lew. Of all the murder cases that happened in this town in the past two years, not one was closed by the local police. They were solved by a woman by the name of Kate Fallon. I've been led to believe by my journalistic source that Miss Fallon is a younger real-life American version of Agatha Christie's fictional amateur female sleuth, Miss Jane Marple."

"If she's that good," said Valentine with a grin, "ask her if she'd like to move to New York and join the NYPD. Tell her for me that we've always got room on the force for another top-notch detective."

The police commissioner looked at his pocket watch.

Aleck sighed. "Surely, you're not thinking about leaving so early?"

"I have to get downtown to headquarters. It's New Year's Eve in New York and I am the police commissioner. Enjoy your trip out of town, and your lunch with the trifecta. As for the city honoring Johnny Groover, I'll suggest it to Hizzoner. But I'm not sure the mayor will take kindly to a proposal that he give the keys to the city to a kid who stuck up a payroll truck, even if he is a certified war hero."

11

POURING TEA INTO delicate antique cups for Kate Fallon and Scrappy MacFarland, Beatrice Bradshaw said, "I don't know which is going to be more exciting to me, the ceremonies welcoming our local hero, or me actually getting to meet the famous Alexander Whiteside. I'll probably be so awed by being in his presence that I won't be able to open my mouth."

"Don't worry about that, Mrs. Bee," said Scrappy. "Aleck will handle all the talking." He plunked a sugar cube into the teacup before him and studied a large porcelain plate heaped with scones she had made for him because they were his favorite of all her baked goods. "Aleck is the gabber of all gabbers. His nonstop loquaciousness during a weekend at the country estate of a friend, the playwright Russell Branson, drove the guests crazy. That long ordeal inspired Russ to write the Broadway comedy hit of 1939, *The House Guest from Hell.*"

"I saw the movie version," said Kate. "It was hilarious, especially the part about the gallstone he had made into a pendant for his watch chain."

"That was not made up. Aleck actually had a gallstone operation. He had it mounted in a gold pendant and wore it as if it was the Hope Diamond. If you don't believe me, I'll send Aleck a wire and tell him to bring the damn thing with him."

Pausing in lifting a teacup, Beatrice said, "I'm glad Mr. Whiteside made a watch fob of his gallstone. It's a nice eccentricity. I like eccentric people. Perhaps it's because I'm English."

"If I may show off my Shakespeare," said Scrappy, " 'Where'er I wander, boast of this I can, though banish'd, yet a true-born Englishman.' In this case, a true-born English *woman*."

"Richard the Second," said Beatrice. Eyes welling with tears, she recited:

> "This royal throne of kings, this scepter'd isle,
> This earth of majesty, this seat of Mars,
> This other Eden, demi-paradise,
> This fortress built by Nature for herself
> Against infection and the hand of war,
> This happy breed of men, this little world,
> This precious stone set in the silver sea,
> Which serves it in the office of a wall,
> Or as a moat defensive to a house,
> Against the envy of less happier hands . . ."

Scrappy gave a nod of his head and interrupted with, "As Herr Hitler quickly discovered, and then changed his mind about trying to invade England."

"'This blessed plot, this earth, this realm,'" Beatrice continued, "'this England.'"

Scrappy grinned. "You and Aleck will get on very well, Bea. He's not only an Anglophile, he claims to have given Churchill the line about Churchill having nothing to offer the English but blood, toil, tears, and sweat. He will also be thrilled to find out that his official hostess when he's here in Robinsville owns a bookstore that has a huge section devoted to mysteries. Aleck considers himself an expert on the genre, and *the* American expert on Sherlock Holmes. He's a cofounder of the preeminent American Sherlockian group, the Baker Street Irregulars."

"I know of his interest in the mystery novel," said Beatrice. "I also read in an article in a magazine that he is a close friend of Rex Stout and claims that he was the inspiration for Stout's detective Nero Wolfe, both intellectually and physically."

"Aleck isn't quite as fat as Wolfe, but he's certainly ample in avoirdupois," said Scrappy. Turning to Kate, he continued, "But what really interests him is real-life murders, so I'm sure he will be interested in hearing you tell him about how you solved a couple of murders right here in little old Robinsville. It's because of Aleck's interest in murder that I met him. I was working the police beat for the old *New York Mirror*. We ran into each other during the Ruth Snyder–Judd Gray case in 1927. Ruth and Judd killed Ruth's husband, Albert, with a sash weight while Albert was sleeping. They figured they'd committed the perfect murder. The cops solved it in under two hours and got confessions from Ruth and Judd in which they blamed each other. Aleck wrote a great piece for his paper with a description of Ruth and Judd in the opening line that I can still quote. 'She's a chilly-looking blond with frosty eyes and a heart as cold and hard as a tombstone in a blizzard and he's as bright as the chunk of iron which they used to clobber poor Albert.' "

"How ghastly," exclaimed Beatrice. "What happened to them?"

"They went to the chair at Sing Sing. First Judd, then Ruth. Aleck was present, of course, but with a small camera hidden under his pants leg and strapped to his ankle. The moment that the switch was thrown, he jerked up the leg and got one picture. It filled the front page of an extra edition of Aleck's paper with a one-word headline: FRIED."

Beatrice put down her cup. "I find it hard to believe that a man of Alexander Whiteside's erudition, the man who speaks on the radio each Sunday evening with such authority, wit, and sensitivity on the fine arts of drama, literature, poetry, and painting, was once a reporter covering grisly murder cases."

"Men and women were killing each other long before they took up painting and writing," said Scrappy with a chuckle as he reached for a scone, "and there's no better training in journalism than crime reporting. Sports writing comes in a close second. That's because in crimes and sports you find the essence of the human condition. What is journalism but the holding up of a mirror to human nature. Good reporting spotlights it whether it's on a baseball diamond, football gridiron, tennis court, and hockey rink or in a bedroom in a house in Queens where some poor sap fell asleep believing that his wife loved him."

Kate asked, "And where does war fit in?"

Lifting the scone to his mouth, Scrappy replied, "War is just a more brutal kind of sport and murder carried out on a bigger scale. In terms of journalism, the challenge in reporting on a war is finding a way to portray it on a human scale. You can say in a story how much tonnage in the form of explosives was droped on the enemy's cities, or you can write about a kid from a small town in Pennsylvania who was given a choice between going to prison for a few years or into the Marine Corps, chose the latter, and became a hero. I can tell you this with certainty. If Johnny Groover's claim to fame was that he was a bombardier who plastered Berlin with bombs, instead of getting shot three times on Guadalcanal, Aleck Whiteside wouldn't be coming down from New York City to preside as master of ceremonies at the homecoming ceremonies which you ladies have been chosen to plan. What have you come up with?"

As Scrappy bit into the scone, Beatrice answered, "We are proposing that the festivities be held in three parts. The first will be a brief ceremony at the railroad station when Johnny's train arrives on Wednesday morning, followed by a procession of automobiles escorting him to his home. Two will be provided by the Harlan Smith auto dealership, including a convertible for Johnny, Mayor Cantrell, and Mr. Whiteside. Three other sedans will be loaned by Ed Polansky."

"Let's hope our esteemed funeral director informs the drivers of the nature of this job," said Scrappy, "or part of the procession will wind up going to the cemetery."

"The second part of the celebration will be an informal affair on Wednesday evening in the junior high school gymnasium," Beatrice continued. "Music for dancing will be provided by the senior high school swing band. Food and drinks, nonalcoholic, will be courtesy of the Vale-Rio Diner and Buster's Restaurant. There will be a head table but no speeches. Those who choose to attend will have to pay for admission by buying a war bond in the amount of fifty dollars."

Having finished eating the scone, Scrappy said, "I look forward to at least one dance with each of you charming ladies."

"The formal program at which Mr. Whiteside speaks and our war hero is to be honored with a presentation by Mayor Cantrell will be held on Thursday evening at eight o'clock in the junior high school auditorium. We thought of having the event at the football field, but we were afraid there could be snow."

"Because you are an old friend of Alexander Whiteside," said Kate to Scrappy, "you are being assigned to see that he is well taken care of during his visit to our town."

"Your first job is to invite him to a home-cooked supper right here in my house with Kate and me, and you, of course. After all, we don't want him going on the air and telling the country that the people of Robinsville are inhospitable, do we? When will he arrive?"

"I'm meeting his ten o'clock train from Philly on Tuesday morning."

12

THE TRAIN ALERTED people on the Robinsville Station platform of its arrival with a plaintive wail of its whistle long before the northwest-bound train could be seen rounding the last curve before the town. Two minutes later, trailing gray smoke and gushing plumes of steam from its sides, the black 4-3-4–wheeled Baldwin-built locomotive slowed and eased to a smooth stop. Behind the engine stretched seven royal blue coaches of the Shamokin Express of the Reading Company's Schuylkill River service. A second later, a conductor and six trainmen stepped down to the platform and offered assistance in detraining to several young men in Army uniforms, each with a duffel bag, two elderly women carrying shopping bags, and a middle-aged man with two heavy suitcases.

Last to appear in a doorway, Alexander Whiteside was wrapped in a raccoon coat that Scrappy MacFarland thought had been out of style since the 1929 Wall Street Crash. With its collar raised, Scrappy could barely discern the owlish face, small gray bristle mustache, and wire-rimmed spectacles. A large, squarish, black fur Russian-style hat looked as if it might have been given to Aleck by Stalin himself during Aleck's 1940 visit to Moscow. He descended the stairs slowly and waited while a following porter brought down two heavy, matched-leather suitcases.

Striding to greet the figure who was surely the most remarkable person ever to step from an arriving train in the history of Robinsville, Scrappy exclaimed, "Aleck! Welcome!"

"MacFarland, you old ink-stained wretch," said Aleck, turning down the collar. "I always assumed when you'd left New York City, presumably to escape either the clutches of an irate husband or the arm of the law, that you had fled to hide out in another metropolis. I figured you would go to Chicago, San Francisco, or even Los Angeles. Life is so full of surprises!"

"I trust you had a nice trip down from Baghdad on the Hudson?"

"To quote my dear friend Edna Saint Vincent Millay, 'There's not a train I wouldn't take, no matter where it's going.' In this case, two trains."

As the train's whistle tooted twice and doors of passenger cars banged shut, Scrappy took the weighty suitcases. "It's good to see you again. Long time, eh?"

"Not on your grandmother's tintype did I ever expect to find you in a whistlestop burg straight out of a John O'Hara novel."

"Robinsville is quite a nice spot, actually," said

Scrappy as the train moved slowly away from the platform. Leading Aleck toward a parking lot and his Plymouth sedan, he continued, "And it's not a whistlestop. Trains that pause here do so several times a day on a set schedule."

Whiteside smiled impishly. "Usually to pick up people who are leaving, of course."

"How is Jack O'Hara these days? Is he still hanging out at the 21 Club and viewing the world sourly through the bottom of a scotch glass?"

"He is indeed. As to that divine bistro on West Fifty-second Street, you are sorely missed by the barkeeps and waiters, but mostly by the inimitable proprietary cousins Jack and Charlie."

The soldiers who had come in on the train were now getting into a George Washington Army Hospital bus. Reaching his car, Scrappy asked, "Speaking of the 21 Club, how are Jack's younger brothers, Mac, Bob, and Pete?"

"All are doing their bit for the war effort by wearing a uniform," Aleck said as Scrappy opened a rear door. "Jack is in the Marines, Bob in the Army Air Corps. I tried to enlist as well, but they inexplicably classified me as 4-F. Apparently they draw the line at taking middle-aged fat men of dubious sexuality who must wear eyeglasses to read a menu. I immediately appealed the outrageous rejection to the commander in chief himself, but Mr. Roosevelt only threw back his head in that patented manner of his way and let out a ringing laugh. I would have carried my plea to Mrs. Roosevelt, but Eleanor was on one of her inspection tours, though only God and she knows where. How is it that you have not found yourself a position in the war government? You seem to me to be an ideal recruit for a spot in the Office of War Information. Or as one of our mutual friend Wild Bill Donovan's cloak-and-dagger boys in the Office of Strategic Services."

Scrappy grunted a laugh. "Me a spy?"

"Why not? As a journalist you always were quite superlative in the snooping department. Instead, you are editor of a small-town paper named, what?"

"It's called the *Independence.*"

As Scrappy placed both suitcases in the rear of the car, Aleck went around to the door on the passenger side. "I assume your position qualifies you as the big fish in this small pond?"

"The job provides a modicum of prestige," Scrappy replied, closing the rear door. "But nothing to equal the celebrity that comes with being heard by millions of people each week on a coast-to-coast radio program. The news that the famous Alexander Whiteside would be coming to Robinsville to officiate at the ceremony for our local war hero set the town on its ear."

Whiteside seemed to puff with pride as he got into the car. "Well, of course it did."

"You'll be staying at the General Washington Hotel," said Scrappy as he got behind the steering wheel. "It's Robinsville's finest."

Whiteside jerked with surprise. "You have more than one hotel?"

Scrappy started the engine. "We've got three. And another is under construction close to the new Army hospital."

"Amazing!"

Backing from the parking space, Scrappy continued,

"They all have rooms with electricity, telephones, private baths, and room service."

Aleck watched as the Army bus departed. "What is that you have arranged concerning the ceremony that's brought me here?"

Driving from the lot, Scrappy said, "The event at which you will preside involves presentations of various gifts from the townspeople to Sergeant Groover. You do not make a big speech. It will be held Thursday night in the auditorium of Memorial Junior High School. It's the biggest indoor space available. The organizing committee's first thought was to have the event at the football field, but it being winter, we didn't want to risk inclement weather."

Aleck stroked his fur coat. "Very prudent of you."

"The *main* event involving you," said Scrappy as he stopped to look for traffic before leaving the station, "is to be a more informal reception in the form of a buffet dinner to be held at the Memorial High gymnasium tomorrow evening. That's where you are to present the kid with the letter from FDR inviting him to the White House to receive the Medal of Honor. You did bring the letter?"

Whiteside patted his side. "It's tucked into my inside jacket pocket."

The car turned into the street. "There are no speeches at the reception."

"When do I meet the returning hero?"

"Tomorrow afternoon at a welcoming rally at the railway station when Johnny arrives from Philadelphia. The speakers at that event will be the mayor; myself; the chairman of the festivities, Mrs. Bradshaw; and her assistant, Kate Fallon."

Aleck turned abruptly. "Ah, that's the person whom I am really eager to meet. I daresay that getting to talk with the young woman who solves murders in her spare time is of much more interest to me than taking part in the ceremonies for your homegrown hero. I intend to do a radio broadcast about her, perhaps two. I'm counting on you to arrange for me to interview this Miss Fallon . . . at length."

"I can't guarantee you an interview. Kate's a very modest gal. But you'll meet her this evening. She and her friend Beatrice Bradshaw have invited you to supper at Bea's house. You'll like Bea. She owns the town's bookstore and is a great fan of Alexander Whiteside."

"I like her already. Tell me more about Kate Fallon."

"After her fiancée went into the army, she quit working as a typist in the general office of the steel mill and took a job in a defense plant. She's a welder for a firm that machines parts for guns for tanks and fighter planes."

With a clap of pudgy hands, Whiteside exclaimed, "What a woman!"

"She'll be quick to remind you that there are thousands of women all over the country who have gone to work in defense plants."

"Yes, yes, we all know that the nation is brimming with Rosie the Riveters. Admirable! But as far as I know, only one of those patriotic ladies also goes around solving murder cases."

"Aleck," said Scrappy as they arrived at the General Washington Hotel, "I thought your purpose in coming to Robinsville was to shine your spotlight on a kid named Johnny Groover."

"And so I shall, my friend. But as you know, in the universe of radio I am renowned for presenting human interest stories, not to mention my deserved reputation as *the* authority on the topic of murder in America. Now, thanks to the heroics of a young man on the far-off island of Guadalcanal, I find myself in the position of recording several contemporary killings in a small town by interviewing the person who solved them—not a professional sleuth, mind you, but a young woman whose occupation is that of welder in a defense plant! They couldn't come up with a story like that in Hollywood!" He gazed at the hotel and sighed. "It's not exactly the Waldorf-Astoria, is it?"

"Your home-cooked supper will be ready at seven. I'll pick you up at half past six."

A Pause in the Story to Ruminate on Life

REALIZING THAT AT some point during his narrative the cigar he'd been holding had gone out, Scrappy gazed down at it in his hand for so long that I was afraid his mind had wandered far afield and might not return to the subject that had brought me to see him.

As the silence continued, I wondered if he'd stopped talking because he was ill or felt too tired to go on. I asked anxiously, "Is everything all right?"

He responded with a shrug.

"If you'd rather not continue," I said, "just tell me and I'll leave you in peace."

He raised the cigar to eye level. "Have you ever considered the proposition that the noble stogie is a perfect metaphor for life itself?"

I'd been listening to his story while slouched on the bed. Sitting up, I replied, "I'm not a cigar aficionado."

He looked astonished. "How can you possibly be a reporter and not smoke cigars?"

"Even if I did, smoking's not allowed in the city room."

Shaking his head, he muttered, "No wonder journalism has gone to hell."

Standing to stretch, I asked, "When was the last time you were in a newsroom?"

"I don't remember," he said, balancing the cigar on the edge of a table next to his chair. "It's been quite a while. Years. A couple of decades, maybe. But when I was there, nobody dared to tell me to put out my cigar."

"Today there would be no place to discard it. There are no ashtrays!"

"Well, there's always the floor."

I shook my head. "It's carpeted."

"Carpeting in a city room?"

"Times have changed. You wouldn't recognize your old bailiwick. It's a computerized place now. My copy goes straight from my computer to the editor, and from his it goes right to the computer in the press room. There are no typewriters, no linotype machines. Most of the time the place is as quiet as a hospital."

Rising slowly from his chair, he picked up the cigar and muttered, "You make it seem more like a morgue. Now you'll have to excuse me for a minute. I have to take a leak and get rid of this dead soldier."

He disappeared into the adjacent bathroom. When he returned, he declared, "Forget what Coca-Cola says in its advertising. The pause that refreshes is a good piss." The cigar was gone. "I always flush the carcasses of my stogies," he explained. "If I don't, the snippy orderly that comes in to straighten up my room in the evenings gives me a dirty look and a lecture about how I am, quote, *stinking up the place,* unquote. But he has a point. There's nothing pretty about a dead cigar."

"Is that what you mean about a cigar as a metaphor for life itself?"

"When did I say that?"

"Just now."

He sank into his chair. "A curious thing about being my age is that I can't always recall what happened a few minutes ago, yet I remember events of fifty years ago as if they happened only yesterday. I suppose that's God's way of reminding us that we are all sinners."

"Well, I'm grateful that you've got such a clear recall of the Groover murder case."

Lifting the second cigar from the table where he'd laid it, he gave me an impatient look. "My short-term memory may be sporadic, young man, but I'm pretty sure I have not yet used the word *murder* in my narrative in relation to Johnny Groover."

I grinned. "I note that you said *not yet.*"

"You surprise me, young man. You don't strike me as the kind of person who becomes so impatient when he's reading a mystery novel that he skips to the end to find out who done it."

"I'm not."

"Then please hold your horses now."

"I'm sorry."

"You were sent here not just to learn about the mysterious death of Johnny Groover and how it happened. Your assignment is to find out why the circumstances of it have been, to use a phrase that is so popular with your tenacious boss, *covered up.*"

"This is true. As we in the news business have been saying since the days of the Nixon Watergate scandal, it's not the crime, it's the cover-up."

"There was another significant maxim coined at that time, by Tricky Dick himself as I remember: 'Follow the money.'"

I smiled and resumed my place on the bed. "For a moment there I thought you were going to say, 'I am not a crook.'"

"Why should that statement spring to your mind?"

"Johnny Groover was involved in the payroll robbery, right?"

"Oh sure!"

"It occurred to me as you were talking about the robbery that it might turn out he wasn't part of it, or that he'd somehow been set up."

"There was never any doubt that Johnny was involved in that little Coldstream Road caper up to his neck," Scrappy said, performing the lighting ritual with the second cigar. "Now where did I leave off?"

"Aleck Whiteside had been invited to supper by Beatrice Bradshaw and Kate Fallon."

"We had Virginia baked ham. How Bea managed to find one when meat was rationed is still a mystery. It was a nice supper, enjoyed by all. Aleck was thrilled to learn that Bea owned a bookstore."

"What did he think of Kate Fallon?"

"Everyone who met Kate was immediately enthralled with her."

"How old was Kate's brother Paul at the time of the Groover case?"

"There you go again. Did I ever say there was a

Groover *case*? In 1943 Paulie was about nine years old. He and Kate were very close. In a big family the oldest and the youngest usually are, but I think Kate and Paulie grew especially close because of Kate's fella being away in the army. Paulie helped her deal with her loneliness."

"What did you think of him?"

"When your current boss was nine years old, he was as big a pain in the ass as he is now, always butting in, asking questions. I suppose that's why he wound up being a newsman. But in getting back to Johnny Groover, we jump ahead now—two days—with the town all decked out in red-white-and-blue bunting and eagerly awaiting the arrival of Johnny's train."

Part 2

The Homecoming

"Oh Look at Me Now."

—Popular hit in 1941 by the
TOMMY DORSEY ORCHESTRA

13

TWO MINUTES AFTER the Reading Railroad's 9:20 A.M. Pottsville Express left the station at Norristown, it came to a high, slightly curving trestle spanning the Schuylkill River. Feeling self-conscious in the blue Marine Corps dress tunic with its high collar, USMC insignia, its line of brass buttons, red-and-gold sergeant chevrons, and lighter blue pants with red stripes, Johnny Groover was acutely aware of sympathetic looks from other passengers who'd watched him as he used a cane to board the train at Philadelphia's Reading Terminal. Looking down at the ice-clogged water under the bridge, he muttered, "Next stop, Robinsville."

Seated beside him on the aisle in crisp Navy officer whites, Lieutenant Dino Minetta asked, "Feeling nervous?"

Johnny turned away from the window. "The word I'd use is *silly.*"

"There's nothing silly in being a hero."

"Hey, I'm no hero," Johnny whispered, but forcefully. "I know it, you know it, and the president damn well ought to know it."

The lieutenant replied softly, "The president knows what he chooses to know."

Johnny fingered the curved handle of the brown cane. "All the heroes are the guys who are still out there."

"Right now the people need to see one up close."

"No wonder you got picked to escort me home," said Johnny, facing Minetta. "You are one hell of a gung-ho officer! I admire your ability to keep a straight face. As for me, I feel like a fool in these dress blues. I could've worn my regular uniform. I look like a recruiting poster."

"I think that's the point. Or part of it."

"Except for the cane, of course."

"You know what, Johnny? I'm getting kind of tired of this sack cloth and ashes routine. When are you going to ditch the 'Oh Dear Lord, why I am alive when so many better men than me are dead?' crap? You're a sergeant in the Marines and you've been given a job to do, so shut your yap about being unworthy and go with the flow."

Johnny's hand rose from the cane and snapped a salute. "Yes, sir, Lieutenant, *sir*."

"When the spotlight goes off, you can put in for another combat tour and proceed to get your head blown off, if that's what you believe you deserve."

The hand returned to the cane. "Maybe I will."

"But for now, you are *it* in the hail-the-hero department," said Minetta, voice rising, "so grit your teeth and do your duty. After all, it's nothing really new for you, is it?"

"What are you talking about?"

"When this train pulls in and you see all the people on

the platform, pretend it's another high school football pep rally and you are again the star quarterback of the Robinsville . . . what's the team's name?"

Johnny grinned. "The Robinsville High School Phantoms."

"Well, rah-rah-rah."

"Did you ever play?"

"Football?"

"Yeah."

"I gave it a shot."

"What position?"

"I was right end."

"Were you any good?"

"Till the day I broke an ankle."

"That's tough."

"Not as tough as catching several Jap bullets."

"How did you wind up in the Navy?"

"I enlisted. I prefer sleeping on clean sheets to muddy foxholes."

As the train left the trestle, made a sharp turn for a straight run to the north, and picked up speed, Johnny said, "Minetta. You're Italian, so you must be Catholic. I've heard it's a hard religion. Is it?"

"*Life* is hard."

"Tell me about having to confess your sins to a priest."

A conductor appeared. Touching the brim of his cap with a two-finger salute, he smiled and asked, "Is everything okay, fellas? Comfortable, Sergeant?"

"Just fine," Johnny answered. "When do we get to Robinsville?"

"We'll be there in about fifteen minutes. When I came through there this morning on the way to Philly, the station was all decked out for your welcoming ceremony. I expect you'll find a big crowd waiting to greet you. I speak for the train's crew when I say that we're proud to have you on board, Sergeant."

As the conductor walked forward in the coach calling for tickets of anyone who'd gotten on at Norristown, Johnny looked out the window at familiar landmarks. Each meant how far he was in miles and time from the hometown and the people in it that he thought he would never see again. Presently, storage sheds painted with the name BROWNBACK LUMBER CO., stacks of plywood sheets, and mountains of planks rushed past the window. They meant that the train would slow down in anticipation of the last curve in the line before Robinsville, only three miles and about five minutes away.

Almost two years had passed since he'd boarded a train going to Philadelphia to join the Marines. His orders said that he would be met at the Reading Terminal by a Marine sergeant who would escort him to the Pennsylvania Railroad's 30th Street Station and another train with a special car to take Marine recruits to the boot camp at Parris Island, South Carolina. The only person to see him off as he left Robinsville that day had been his father. They had stood in the bitter cold without saying a word until his train stopped. And then only nine words: "You take care of yourself, boy." "Don't worry, Pop."

Turning from the window, Johnny glowered at Lieutenant Minetta. "Whose crazy idea was it to have a damn welcoming ceremony at the train station?"

Lieutenant Minetta raised his hands defensively. "I assure you it wasn't me!"

14

HALF AN HOUR before the Pottsville Express was due, Kate Fallon had watched as Beatrice Bradshaw gazed at herself in a dressing table mirror in her bedroom. Assessing the propriety of a small blue bonnet that she'd adorned with three small paper American flags and two larger Union Jacks, Beatrice asked, "Do you think I'm overdoing it with this hat?"

"It's perfect."

"Are you sure Mayor Cantrell understands that there are to be *no* long speeches?"

"His Honor understands he's to say only a few words of welcome. Stop worrying. It's all going to proceed exactly as planned. When the train stops, the band strikes up 'When Johnny Comes Marching Home.' Johnny leaves the train and is met by Scrappy MacFarland. He escorts him to the speaker's platform, where he's greeted by Coach Franklin and a few members of the teams Johnny played on. The junior high school band plays the National Anthem, Monsignor Federico of St. Ann's Church delivers the invocation, then the senior high school band plays the Phantoms' Fight Song, and the mayor gives his welcome speech. Reverend Holland of St. John's Lutheran Church gives a brief benediction. After that, Johnny rides through downtown in a convertible with his father and the Navy officer who's been assigned to accompany him. They go to the Groover house on the north side."

With a worried frown, Beatrice said, "I think we've made a mistake in not providing for a few remarks by Mr. Whiteside."

"Aleck is quite content to speak at the formal ceremony. He told me that if he were to make a speech at a railroad station, he would feel as though he were a shill for the Ringling Brothers Circus, or worse, a politician running for election."

Giving a final glance at the reflection of the flag-festooned bonnet and donning a black overcoat, Beatrice announced, "I'm ready. I just hope I'm not going to look so silly that I'll be a complete laughingstock."

As Kate followed Beatrice out the door, Chief of Police Detwiler was seated at his desk at police headquarters. The last time he'd worn his full-dress uniform to welcome someone to town had been on a blazing-hot August afternoon in 1940 for a whistle-stop speech by the Republican candidate for president, Wendell Wilkie.

A dark-horse contender at the GOP convention that year in Philadelphia, he had gotten the nomination on the sixth ballot. With the delegates deadlocked between Governor Thomas E. Dewey and Senator Robert A. Taft, Wilkie forces had stampeded the weary delegates by packing the galleries with supporters who'd chanted "We want Wilkie." He'd arrived in Robinsville on a special three-car train and resembled a Bridge Street merchant in a rumpled gray suit. Speaking briefly from the open platform of the private Pullman of the president of the Reading Line, he had a raspy voice. Constantly brushing back errant strands of his shock of unruly dark hair, he'd warned the hardworking people of Robinsville that if FDR won an unprecedented third term, they would soon see their sons marching to war.

The large crowd that turned out to see Wilkie had come for just that purpose—to have a look at a man who was running for president. But when they went to the polls in November, they cast their votes for President Roosevelt by a margin of four-to-one.

There'd been an even larger turnout for a welcoming ceremony at the Reading Station in September 1942. The attraction on that day had been a group of movie stars. Urging the people of the town to buy war bonds were Judy Garland; Mickey Rooney; Alexis Smith; Bette Davis; and Greer Garson and Walter Pidgeon, stars of the popular war movie *Mrs. Miniver.* A further enticement to the people of the town to buy bonds was a special showing that night of the movie at the Colonial Theater. The admission price for an adult was the purchase of a bond. Kids got in if they bought a half-dollar's worth of War Savings Stamps.

None of these previous occasions had involved arranging for a parade through the town. There were two parades a year in Robinsville—the Dogwood Festival in June and on the Fourth of July—but to handle this one, plus the welcoming ceremony at the train station, had required him to not only cancel all days off for members of the force, but borrow six officers from Spring City and Royersford to man posts at downtown intersections. The only time there had been such a large motorcade was for the funeral of Amanda Burford Griffith. The send-off for her had been big not only because she had been the major stockholder in the Robinsville Steel Company and benefactress of numerous charities, but because the gracious old lady had been murdered.

Assured by Todd Doebling that every man assigned to the Groover parade was in place along the route and at the railway station, and informed by officials of the Reading Railroad that the train carrying Johnny Groover was on time, Detwiler gave an emphatic nod of his head.

Reaching for his heavily gold-braided blue hat, he said, "Okay, let's get this show on the road. After all, it's not every day that we're called on to lead a parade for a certified war hero we once did our best to lock up."

"I know that case is still eating at you, Chief," said Doebling, following Detwiler out the door, "but in my opinion the money left town with Pete Slattery."

"If we ever find him," Detwiler grumbled as he strode toward his car, "and if we give him a damned parade and the keys to the city, maybe he'll tell us what he did with it."

After a restless night, Mrs. Josephine Perillo had risen at half past five to attend the first daily mass at St. Ann's. Because it was held at six o'clock for the men whose shift at the steel plant started at seven, it was called the Working Man's Mass. But since the war started, most of the Faithful in the pews were women whose husbands, sons, and brothers had gone off to fight it.

Mrs. Perillo's purpose in attending this morning was to speak to the Monsignor in the hope of talking him out of taking part in the welcoming ceremony at the station for the Groover boy. Seated at the rear of the church with her overcoat on, she held a large handbag and waited anxiously for the Mass to begin. Disappointed when the celebrant who appeared at the altar was Father Brennan, she hurried from the church without genuflecting. Going to the front door of the parish house, she hoped to speak to the Monsignor there.

Her knocks were answered by a nun. After listening to her request to see the Monsignor, she replied, "He's not in. He's downtown having an early breakfast at the General Washington Hotel with Mr. MacFarland from the newspaper and Mr. MacFarland's guest from New York, Mr. Alexander Whiteside, the famous radio broadcaster. The Monsignor will be back after the welcoming ceremony at the station for Sergeant Groover. If you can come back after lunchtime, the Monsignor will be glad to see you."

"Thank you, Sister," said Josephine, "but that will be too late."

"If it's an urgent problem, Father Brennan can see you after Mass."

"No, thank you," said Josephine, walking away.

Breakfast in the dining room of the General Washington Hotel had been scrambled eggs and thin, crisply fried scrapple doused with catsup. After explaining to Aleck Whiteside that scrapple was a kind of sausage that came in blocks rather than links, and that one would be wise not to ask what it was made of, Scrappy MacFarland opined, "While some aficionados of the unique Pennsylvania dish swear that it should be drowned in maple syrup, I prefer ketchup."

Turning to Monsignor Federico, Aleck asked, "And what is the stance of the Roman Catholic Church on the scrapple question?"

"As long as it's not eaten on Friday or any of the meatless holy days," the Monsignor replied, "the Holy See has adopted no position vis-à-vis syrup or catsup."

After a tenuous taste of the brownish-gray meat, Aleck said, "It is certainly unique. And not as bad as its name suggests."

"Excuse me if I'm being too personal, Mr. Whiteside," said the Monsignor while Aleck scooped more scrapple onto his plate, "but are you a religious man?"

"Not by your standards, I'm sure, Monsignor."

"Are you religious by anyone's standards?"

"I heartily approve of Christmas."

"Do you refer to the secular trappings of the holiday, or to its true meaning?"

"I'm all for giving gifts to children, following the Golden Rule, glad tidings, and all the Charles Dickens stuff. And I never fail to devote an entire broadcast to the retelling of the story of the Babe of Bethlehem. However, if you are asking if I'm a Christian and if by being one you mean have I taken part in a baptismal ceremony, I do not qualify."

The Monsignor's eyes went wide with shock. "You've not been baptized?"

"My mother was a member of the North American Phalanx. It was a sect established in the middle years of the last century in upstate New York that was more agricultural than religious. And more communist than capitalist. However, my dear friend Heywood Broun, who is a newspaperman of some repute, has lately been trying to get me to convert to Catholicism. He is assisted in this enterprise by the playwright Clare Boothe Luce. Both have been joined in this conspiracy by an especially persuasive man of the cloth and Roman collar with a mellifluous voice and the most piercing eyes ever to look into a man's soul. He's also a Monsignor. His name is Fulton J. Sheen. Their most recent assault on my paganism took place just a few weeks ago in, of all places, the bar room of the 21 Club. Rather an odd place to be talking about bringing somebody to Jesus Christ, wouldn't you say?"

"Our Blessed Lord is interested in saving souls no matter where he finds them. I know of Monsignor Sheen through his great work with the Society for the Propagation of the Faith. I try not to miss his weekly radio programs."

"Do you ever tune in to mine?"

"When I learned from Mr. MacFarland that 'The Voice of the People' would be taking part in this week's events in honor of Sergeant Groover, I imposed upon him to arrange for me to meet you. His price for arranging this delightful breakfast was my agreement to give the opening prayer at this morning's welcoming ceremony. I promise not to drag it out. I'm sure the people at the train station will be eager to hear you speak."

"They're going to be disappointed," said Scrappy. "Aleck's big moment comes later in the week."

"It will give the people of Robinsville something to look forward to," said Aleck.

"Don't underestimate the resourcefulness of people in a small town in finding ways to keep their lives interesting, Mr. Whiteside. They don't have a glamorous 21 Club to go out to on Saturday night, or stage shows to see at a Radio City Music Hall and a Paramount Theater, but they are not a bunch of hicks in the sticks. The young men of Robinsville who have been taken from their homes to fight this war are not like the doughboys of the First World War. No one is going to sing of this crop of small-town boys, 'How you gonna keep 'em down on the farm after they've seen Paree?'"

"You're right, Monsignor, that was a snobbish crack. My numerous critics don't call me Smart Aleck for no reason. I apologize."

"Aleck is interested in doing a broadcast about one resident of our little town," Scrappy interjected, "who's found a way to fight the war from right here . . . and the time, now and then, to solve murder cases."

The Monsignor smiled broadly. "Ah, yes, our indomitable Kate Fallon!"

Finished with his breakfast, Aleck asked, "Is she one of your flock, Monsignor?"

"Although the name *Fallon* is Irish, Kate and her family are Episcopalians."

Reaching for his cup of coffee, Aleck said, "Well, that's *almost* Catholic, isn't it?"

"On that provocative note, gentlemen," said Scrappy, looking at his wristwatch, "I think we'd best pile into my 1938 Plymouth that's going to have to last me for the duration of the war and get ourselves down to the train station; otherwise, I'll never find a place to park it."

15

MORNINGS FOR RALPH Franklin in all his years as the coach of the Robinsville Phantoms had been an unaltered routine. After his jog around the neighborhood, he took a short, cold shower. Wearing only a white undershirt and boxer shorts, he went into kitchen for a small bowl of Kellogg's corn flakes without sugar and a large cup of black coffee. Spread before him was the sports page of the *Independence*. At half past seven he returned to his bedroom to put on a pair of navy blue calf-length socks, a white shirt with a plain necktie, and a gray or brown double-breasted suit. A sweat suit and athletic shoes for the afternoons when he coached the football team were kept in one of his lockers in his office in the field house at Washington Field.

But on this brisk morning he would not be spending his day teaching hygiene to boys at Robinsville High School. By order of the school board president, the students in all the town's schools had been given the day off so that they could attend the welcoming ceremony at the train station for Johnny Groover.

At the request of the organizers of the reception, Kate Fallon and Beatrice Bradshaw, the man who'd coached Johnny would be joined on stage by a few draft-exempt former Phantoms team members who had played in Johnny's games. They would all ride behind him in open cars in the subsequent parade.

A triple banner headline of the *Independence* blared:

THE BIG DAY IS HERE; THOUSANDS EXPECTED
TO WELCOME HOME OUR HEROIC MARINE;
HUGE PARADE WILL FOLLOW HIS ARRIVAL

A large photo of an appropriately warrior-looking Johnny Groover in his formal Marine uniform was placed in the middle of the page above the fold. It was surrounded by a group of smaller pictures of Johnny in action on the gridiron. Another showed Johnny surrounded by the 1940 Phantoms all-star backfield. Scrappy MacFarland had named them "The Fabulous Four." Kneeling with a ball in his hands, Johnny was surrounded by Larry Smith, Dave Kolker, and Pete Slattery. Another photo was Johnny accepting the trophy awarded that year to the most valuable player in the county scholastic football league.

Omitted from the display, Franklin noted with relief, was the photograph of Johnny on the day he was arrested for complicity in the payroll robbery. Looking terrified, he was snapped by Scrappy MacFarland being led out of the field house by Chief Detwiler and Officer Todd Doebling.

Expecting to be taken into custody, but not wanting to subject his father to the scandal and humiliation of seeing his son arrested, Johnny had chosen to wait for the police at the place where he'd always sought solace and comfort in dealing with the problems of a boy on his way to becoming a man.

According to Scrappy MacFarland's prediction in his front-page story on plans for the welcome at the Reading Station, the triumphal parade through downtown, and the events at the junior and senior high schools later in the week, Johnny would find himself basking in the same kind of cheers and adulation that he'd experienced in four years of playing ball for the Robinsville Phantoms.

Gazing proudly at the front page of the newspaper, Franklin decided that the picture he liked most was of a grinning, grimy, sweating Johnny Groover standing in front of the field house lockers after the team's 1940 runaway defeat of Robinsville's arch-rivals, the Kenington Kings. Barechested, he had an arm around the shoulders of Richie Zale.

The caption read: "The dazzling teamwork of quarterback Johnny Groover and indispensable open-field blocker Richard Zale caused four seasons of victory-hungry Robinsville football fanatics to compare the daring duet of the Washington Field gridiron with another pair of flashy fighters, the 'dynamic duo' of comic books and a movie serial 'Batman and Robin.' "

Still in his work clothes, Richie Zale had toast and coffee alone in the kitchen. He'd come home from the overnight shift at the steel plant and found Mildred giving him the silent treatment. As cold as ice, she'd declared, "You'll have to get your own breakfast. I've got a headache, so I'm going back to bed for a while. I don't want to be disturbed. You'll find the clothes you'll be wearing for your big moment in the limelight with your pal Johnny Groover in the bathroom."

With rising anger, he demanded, "Does this mean you're not taking the kids to the station and the parade?"

"I have no intention of dragging them downtown just to stand around in the cold."

"Okay, then I'll take them along with me."

"If you do," she said, "you'll find your bags packed when you get back."

Grabbing her arms, he shouted, "This is crazy! *You're* crazy."

Wrenching free, she strode toward the stairs. Pausing before going up, she declared, "By the way, have you seen the morning paper? You'll find it on the kitchen table. There's a picture of you and Johnny together on the front page with your arms around each other."

Picking up the paper and looking at the photo, he said, "For cripes sake, Millie, you have to let go of this nutty idea that Johnny and I were—"

"As I said, you'll find your change of clothes laid out in the bathroom."

Back in the kitchen, he picked up the newspaper, stared at the photographs, and muttered, "Johnny, you tough son of a bitch, I think we'd all be better off if one of those Jap soldiers had killed you."

Entering his sister's bedroom in the uniform of the Robinsville High School Dancing Band, Nancy Roberts found Patricia standing before a mirror in a new red dress.

Her face was scrunched in a disapproving expression. "This looked so much better on me when I tried it on in the store," she announced. "Now it makes me look dumpy."

"Then don't wear it," said Nancy, leaning in the doorway. "If you haven't worn it, you can take it back and exchange it for another color. Or you could give it to me."

"I bought it because red is Bobby Gordon's favorite color. He's been picked to be one of the honor guards at the ceremony for Johnny Groover. When it's over, and he's off duty, we're going to have lunch at the General Washington Hotel."

Nancy came up straight. "Wow. That's a pretty expensive place on an Army corporal's pay, isn't it? What's the reason for this splurge?"

Pat turned with a widening grin. "Little sister, this could be *the* day that Bobby pops the big question."

"Oh muhgod," Nancy exclaimed, throwing herself onto her back on the bed.

"I had a feeling he was on the verge the other night, but I guess he decided that a booth at the Vale-Rio Diner wasn't the proper place."

"Life sure can be cruel."

"What are you talking about?"

"I was thinking about poor Johnny Groover," said Nancy, gazing up at the ceiling. "First, the guy gets a Dear John letter from you, then almost gets killed three times, and now, on the exact same day that he's coming home as a hero, the girl he loves is getting engaged."

"If Johnny was ever in love with me, he's gotten over it by now, I'm sure."

Nancy sat up. "Suppose he didn't get your letter. Suppose he's coming home with an engagement ring for you in his pocket?"

"Don't be ridiculous," said Pat as she put on the red dress. "The trouble with you, little sister, is that you see too many romantic movies."

Exactly at 6:00 A.M., with the first of the daytime employees arriving for work at the Graf & Son Movers and Fireproof Storage Co. warehouse on Front Street, Delmer Turner inserted his card into the slot of the time clock. Each walk through the cavernous building every hour on the hour took him fifteen minutes. The other forty-five were passed doing crossword puzzles in the office adjacent to the front door that in the daytime belonged to the warehouse manager, Russ Lamb. Perched on the big desk was a portable Philco radio that Delmer brought from his home each night and kept tuned to the Robinsville station. Operated by the man who also owned the town's piano, musical instrument, and record store, it played classical music until 5:30. The next fifteen minutes were allotted to "Morning Sermon" by a rotating roster of town clergymen. This was followed by ten minutes of recorded sacred music and five minutes of local news direct from the city room of the *Independence*.

The man who presented the news was usually Dick Levitan. Best known to the readers of the paper for colorful reports on the activities at City Hall and the police station, his gruff voice and rapid delivery of the items was a welcome contrast to the smooth tones of most announcers, and in some ways, perhaps deliberately so, similar to the breathless pace of Walter Winchell's news broadcasts on Sunday nights. But in Delmer's opinion, neither man was as good in telling the news as his favorite, Gabriel Heatter, heard on Sunday nights at a quarter to nine. Sponsored by Barbasol shaving cream, he was famous for boosting the morale of listeners in the darkest times of the war by finding some item that would let him say, "Ah, there's good news tonight."

Dick Levitan's news broadcasts usually consisted of a variety of items taken from that day's newspaper, but on this morning he'd devoted the five minutes to the schedule of events in which the town would honor Sergeant Johnny Groover. He signed off his program by saying, "I hope to see you all at the Reading Station or along the route of the big parade."

Switching off the radio, Delmer bitterly noted that there had been no mention of the fact that before Johnny Groover became a war hero, he'd been part of a gang in an armed robbery that had resulted not only in the theft of fifty thousand dollars, but in the driver of the truck that they stuck up losing the best job he'd ever held.

16

As the Pottsville Express glided to a stop at Robinsville, precisely on schedule at 8:47 A.M., the combined junior and senior high schools bands drowned out the hissing steam jetting from the locomotive and cheers from the crowd by playing "When Johnny Comes Marching Home."

Passengers for Robinsville, six in all, left the train first, as arranged, then happily joined the crowd to wait for the appearance of the young hometown man they'd come to hail. Rising above the heads of those at the back of the enthusiastic throng were several placards offering welcome-home sentiments that had been hand-painted by Miss Brownback's third-grade class at the Gay Street Elementary School. Other students waved small American flags.

When Sergeant Johnny Groover appeared in the open doorway of the second car from the end of the train and the two bands broke into "The Marine's Hymn," he reacted by going into a stiff stance and raising a rigid hand to the black visor of his dress-blue cap in a salute. As the music ended and the hand dropped to his side, using a cane, he descended the steps, followed by a young Navy officer.

Awaiting them at the bottom of the stairs was a semi-circle of men with hands extended in the hope of shaking his. Stepping forward and claiming the honor by clasping both the hand and the arm, Mayor Cantrell exclaimed, "On behalf of the proud people of Robinsville, I extend you a heartfelt welcome home!"

Searching the faces, Johnny asked, "Where's my dad?"

"He's waiting for you at home," the mayor answered.

Johnny frowned. "Why isn't he here? Is he sick?"

"I assure you he's feeling fine. He wants to welcome you home without being surrounded by a big crowd. And you can see, it *is* a big one. Probably the biggest we ever had."

Turning to Minetta, Johnny said, "I wasn't really expecting anything close to this. You should've warned me, Lieutenant."

"People love a hero, kid," Minetta. replied. "Just relax and go with the flow."

Still gripping Johnny's arm, the mayor said, "Now, Johnny, let's see if we can make our way over to the speaker's platform."

With a look of alarm, Johnny asked Minetta, "Am I going to have to say something?"

As the crowd broke into another cheer, Minetta had to shout. "Just tell 'em thanks and that you're happy to be home."

With a hand that felt as tight as a vise on Johnny's arm,

the mayor pushed through the crowd as other members of the official greeting committee ordered, "Make way, folks, make way, clear a path, let him through, please."

Upon reaching the red-white-and-blue bunting-draped speaker's platform, Johnny was pleased to find Scrappy MacFarland at the top of the stairway.

"Welcome home, Johnny," he said with a bear hug. "We're all proud of you."

"Thanks, Mr. MacFarland, but is there any way you can get me the hell out of here?"

"Afraid not, Johnny. The whole town's got the day off because of you. After this, there's a parade up Bridge Street. Now, say hello to the folks who have arranged the events of today, and some friends of yours that they thought you'd want to be here."

After Scrappy presented Kate Fallon and Beatrice Bradshaw; radio's famous commentator Alexander Whiteside, who was there, Scrappy explained, to interview him and speak at a later ceremony; Richie Zale; and Coach Franklin, Mayor Cantrell began the ceremony.

As it proceeded, Johnny gazed at the crowd and saw other familiar faces. Many were girls he'd known in school and dated. He saw teachers who'd regarded him as a troublemaker who would never amount to a hill of beans in the world. A few of the men he had known in the various jobs he'd held while in high school. Friends of his father were there, and people from his neighborhood. But two people he saw he had not expected to turn out to welcome him.

In the middle of the throng was Pat Roberts. As beautiful as ever and wearing a red dress, she was standing next to a young man in an Army uniform who had an arm around her shoulder.

Farther back, but still close enough to exhibit her bitter face, was Mrs. Perillo.

Following the ceremony at the station, he saw hundreds of other people whom he did not know. Lining Bridge Street for the parade, they cheered and waved at him. A few women blew kisses at him. Some tossed small bunches of flowers. Many strangers shouted, "Hey, Johnny, welcome home" and "Glad to see ya," as if they were old friends.

Presently, the parade reached the north side and he found himself in the house he grew up in, and which he'd left in disgrace. He found his dad slumped in his favorite chair in the parlor. "So you're back," he said without getting up.

"Yeah."

"Just like a bad penny."

17

"THE BOOK NOOK," said Aleck Whiteside as he, Kate, and Beatrice Bradshaw arrived in front of Beatrice's store after the parade. "You've chosen an apt name for your emporium," he continued as they entered. "It's quaint and to the point."

When she switched on the lights, he found three walls lined with bookcases and several tables stacked with the latest titles.

"Can you think of a more inviting panorama," he asked as he threw open his arms as if he were trying to embrace the room, "than virgin volumes? And there's the delicious aroma of fine papers and good ink. To me there is no greater pleasure than opening a new book, except, of course, opening an old one that you've read many times."

"What we all need right now is some tea," said Beatrice, doffing overcoat and flag-festooned hat as she entered the kitchenette at the back of the store. "I was afraid that if the parade lasted a minute longer, we'd all freeze to death."

"I thoroughly enjoyed myself," said Aleck, taking off his raccoon coat and draping it over the back of a leather armchair. "I've always been a pushover for displays of patriotism."

"Me too," said Kate as Aleck helped her out of her coat. "Every time I hear 'God Bless America' sung by Kate Smith, the tears start flowing."

"The next time I visit her home at Lake Placid, I'll be sure to tell her."

"You actually know Kate Smith?"

"I know everyone, my dear," said Aleck as he picked up the latest Agatha Christie novel, *Murder in Retrospect*.

"I've just read that one," said Kate. "If you like mysteries, I recommend it highly."

According to the book's flap copy, Christie's foppish, transplanted-to-England, Belgian-born sleuth Hercule Poirot was asked to reopen the sixteen-year-old poisoning death of Amyas Crate. Leafing through the book, he said with a chuckle, "Dear Agatha. She so loves to kill off people with poison. She learned about lethal substances as a nurse, long before she took up her pen. I once teased her about her fascination with deadly concoctions. When I was a guest at her house in London before the war, I found myself coming down with a cold. I accused her of testing out a potion by using me as her guinea pig."

Beatrice emerged from the back room carrying a tray. "Did you like London, Aleck?"

"I am and have always been an Anglophile," he said, taking a teacup and passing it to Kate. "If I'd had my way, we would have joined Britain in the fight against the Nazis in 1939."

"As I'm sure you've discerned from Mrs. Bee's accent, and from the Union Jack that she wore on her hat," said Kate, "she was born in England."

Holding up a cup, Aleck said, "I propose we join in a toast to our British allies."

"Here here," said Beatrice. After a sip, she exclaimed, "And one to the United States."

Toasts completed, Aleck said, "I congratulate you ladies on your success in arranging the day's festivities. I thoroughly enjoyed the parade. I thought the man of the hour looked quite handsome in his dress uniform. He seemed to accept all the fuss with the proper attitudes of patience, fortitude, and modesty that we've come to expect in our heroes. I'm looking forward to Scrappy Mac-Farland introducing us at the reception tomorrow evening. Where is Scrappy, by the way? I was hoping he'd join us after the parade."

"I assume he's hard at work," Kate answered, "writing his story for tomorrow's paper."

Interruption for
a Question

"IN YOUR STORY on the ceremony at the train station and the parade that you wrote for the next day's *Independence*," I said as Scrappy MacFarland paused in his narrative to take a puff of his cigar, "you reported that during the ceremony at the station, someone fainted."

"Oh that! It caused a slight hubbub, so I figured I couldn't leave it out."

"It seemed odd to me that you omitted the name of the person who fainted." Dipping a hand in a pocket, I said, "I brought a clipping of your story. May I read part of it to you?"

He shrugged. "Go ahead."

I read, " 'The festivities were interrupted for a brief moment when a woman in the crowd took ill and fainted. She had to be carried away by two police officers.' "

"That's right."

"Why did you leave out the woman's name?"

"Contrary to what you may have heard about me, young man," Scrappy replied in a tone that I can only describe as huffy, "I do have a heart. I'm a compassionate guy. I thought that the woman had been embarrassed enough by having fainted."

Handing him the yellowed clipping, I said, "When I read this, I felt like Sherlock Holmes concerning the dog that didn't bark in the nighttime."

"In this instance the dog that didn't bark is the absence of her name?"

"And that you chose not to include information about what happened after she fainted. Not a word about why she passed out, and nothing concerning her condition."

"It says right here that she was taken away by two cops. As best I recall, Police Officer Doebling, and another officer whose name escapes me, took her to Robinsville Hospital."

"Yet there was no such person listed in the *Independence*'s notice of hospital admissions that date. I checked."

Scrappy cracked a smile and handed back the clipping. "How much is Paulie Fallon paying you?"

"Three hundred a week."

"What a cheapskate! Tell him I said you're worth four hundred, at least."

"I certainly will."

"A man who reads in a fifty-year-old news story about a woman who was reported to have fainted and then checks the newspaper's hospital admissions listings to see who she was and why she fainted is one hell of a good reporter."

"Who was she, Scrappy?"

"Josephine Perillo."

"Perillo. That's the name of the boys who went to prison for the payroll robbery."

"Two went to state prison, one to a reform school."

"So what happened to Josephine Perillo that day at the train station?"

"She showed up packing her dead husband's pistol in her pocketbook. Fortunately, as she was pulling it out, Doebling spotted it and grabbed her. Since no one else had seen the gun, it was decided to keep the incident hush-hush. We found out later from her neighbor that after Josephine's sons were sent away, she'd become mentally unbalanced. Chief Detwiler made sure she couldn't get a chance to get near Groover again by assigning men to keep watch on her until Groover was safely out of town."

"Was Johnny told of the incident?"

"In retrospect maybe he should have been told. Fifty years later, and considering that he wound up dead, it's easy for you to come around asking why he wasn't guarded. But back then there was no reason for us to believe that he might be in danger from someone else."

"There was plenty of reason to think so."

"And in the twenty-twenty vision of hindsight, you can say there was plenty of reason for Jack Kennedy not to ride through Dallas in an open car. Thirty years ago it would have been smart of Nixon to burn the White House tapes. If Bill Clinton knew what he knows now, he wouldn't have gotten involved with that intern and handed out some of those pardons. If any of us thought back then that anyone other than Josephine Perillo was thinking about killing Johnny Groover, he might be around to take part in all the current nostalgia for the Second World War.

He could have been interviewed by Tom Brokaw for his book on 'the greatest generation.' Instead, he was found a couple of days later lying dead in the middle of Washington Field. It's too bad. There's hardly a day goes by that I don't regret what happened. But as F. Scott Fitzgerald observed, 'Show me a hero and I'll write you a tragedy.'"

"I'm sorry. I wasn't being judgmental."

"Apology accepted. Shall I continue?"

"Please."

"The next event was the reception. It was a big bash at which anyone from the general public who wanted to meet Johnny could do so. It was arranged by Kate and Beatrice and held in the junior high school gym. They had it decorated to look like the saloon in *Casablanca*. Unfortunately, the evening nearly ended in a total disaster."

Part 3

A Night in Casablanca

Hearts full of passion, jealousy and hate.

—"As Time Goes By," music and
lyrics by M. K. JEROME AND
JACK SCHOLL, 1942

18

HOLDING AN UNLIT cigar and occupying a reproduction of a Philadelphia-style Federal Era armchair in the Lafayette Suite of the General Washington Hotel, Scrappy MacFarland watched as Aleck Whiteside's surprisingly slender and nimble fingers fashioned a perfect bow tie.

"I never could get the hang of tying one of those things," said Scrappy, looking down at his plain brown neckwear. "If I have to go somewhere in a tuxedo, I wear a ready-made bow tie that has an adjustable band."

"There's nothing to it," said Aleck, turning away from the mirror. "It's like tying shoes. Do we have time for a small repast before we depart?"

"There'll be a buffet laid out at the event."

Aleck made a sour face. "Finger food! What about libations?"

"Fruit punch, I believe. And soft drinks, of course, provided gratis by the local Coca-Cola distributorship."

"My lord, man," said Aleck as he slipped into a gray brocade vest, "has nobody in this town heard that Prohibition ended in 1933? Thank goodness I thought to bring a flask. We'll fill it at the bar on our way out. What's your poison?"

"I'm a scotch drinker."

"I was thinking of brandy."

Scrappy shrugged. "Any port in a storm." He looked at his wristwatch. "If you wish, we have time for a snort at the bar."

"Capital idea! You can brief me further on the crime-busting exploits of Kate Fallon. I've tried to explore the subject with her, my latest attempt being during the parade. But she brushed me off. She said, and these are her exact words, 'The only person you should care about today is a brave young man named Johnny Groover.' This implacable modesty of hers is getting to be downright infuriating."

"If I'd worked as hard as Kate has in arranging Johnny Groover's homecoming," Scrappy replied as Aleck finished dressing, "I wouldn't want to talk about anything else either."

"Be that as it may, I've found a great story in Kate Fallon," said Aleck, striding to the door, "and I assure you I have no intention of leaving town without obtaining it."

"It will be interesting to see if you succeed. But I want your promise that you won't try getting the story tonight. I won't allow you to mess up the evening she and Beatrice Bradshaw have put together. I mean it, Aleck. The evening's spotlight is for Johnny Groover. Do I hear a 'Roger' on that?"

With jutting jaw, Aleck raised a hand in a salute. "Roger! Over and out!"

They discovered the hotel cocktail lounge crowded but found a small table by a window overlooking Bridge Street. A waitress wearing a long dress that Aleck supposed was intended to resemble an outfit that might have been worn by such a woman in 1776 appeared to take their orders for drinks.

Producing a silver half-pint flask from his jacket pocket, Aleck replied, "Please ask the bartender to fill this with your best cognac, and in the meantime bring my friend a scotch—"

"On the rocks," said Scrappy.

"And I'll have scotch, too, but neat," Aleck said with a smile. As she walked away with the flask, he leaned back in his chair with hands folded across his big belly. "Now, my friend, I want you to set aside your adopted role as promoter of the virtues of this town in which you've chosen to feather your nest. Tell me what you think *really* makes Johnny Groover tick."

"I'm not a psychiatrist, Aleck."

"No, but you are a newspaperman in a small town. Notice that I did not say *small-town newspaperman*. I'm sure you will admit there's a difference. The latter is necessarily the head cheerleader of the community who doesn't want to know which closets contain skeletons. The former is fully aware of everything, but he appreciates that some things are best left unrevealed. Except, of course, when his hand is forced."

"What makes you think there might be a skeleton in Johnny Groover's closet?"

"Why wasn't his father at the station to greet him?"

"As I understand it, he doesn't like being in crowds."

"If my son came home a hero, I'd have crawled from my death bed to be there."

"You're a confirmed bachelor. Unless you've been keeping it from me all these years, you don't have children."

"I suspect there's something awry in the Groover father-son relationship."

"If you're saying that Harry Groover doesn't love his son, you're way off base. I remind you that it was Harry who begged a judge to let Johnny join the Marines rather than go to jail."

"Yet he wasn't there when his son returned home in glory."

Bringing the drinks and the flask, the waitress asked, "Anything else, gents?"

"That will be all, thanks," said Scrappy.

"There's one thing," Aleck exclaimed. "A question, if I may? Were you at the parade?"

"I watched it pass by the hotel," the waitress answered.

"Do you know Johnny Groover?"

"I don't *know* him exactly. He was three years behind me in school."

"Were you surprised when you learned that he was a war hero?"

"Not really. He was always acting like a tough guy, on account of being a big star on the football field. All the girls fell for him, even the ones in my senior class."

"But you didn't?"

"He wasn't my type. I don't go for the athletic type. To them life is nothing but beer and chasing girls. A guy like that turns into a husband who'd rather spend a night out with the boys, instead of being at home with the wife. Johnny Groover was also on the dumb side. I prefer guys with brains."

"Well, to each his own, eh? Or in this case, to each *her* own."

As she returned to the bar, Scrappy asked Aleck, "So what did you learn from her?"

Raising his glass of scotch, he replied with a smile, "Boys will be boys."

"Yeah. And some of them become heroes."

"The English boast that all their wars were won by men who trained on the playing fields of Eton. I suppose you believe that America's wars are won because of football."

"Eisenhower was a star player at West Point, until a knee injury sidelined him for good."

"On such trivial events turns history," said Aleck, peering across the cocktail lounge as a naval officer appeared in the doorway. "Oh, there's the Navy captain who has been assigned to chaperone the man of the hour."

"The term is not *chaperone,* it's *escort,*" said Scrappy, raising a hand and wagging it to invite the officer to join them. "His name is Dino Minetta. He's not a captain. He holds the rank of Lieutenant Junior Grade. That's the equivalent of a first lieutenant in the Army."

Minetta arrived at the table. "Good evening, gentlemen."

"Hello, Lieutenant," said Scrappy. "Will you join us for a drink?"

"Thanks very much. I will."

As Scrappy commandeered an empty chair from the next table, Aleck stood and extended a hand to Minetta. "I'm Alexander Whiteside. Call me Aleck."

"'The Voice of the People,'" said Minetta as they shook hands. "Before the war I was a big fan of the program. Please call me Dino."

Scrappy waved a hand at the waitress. When she came to the table, he said, "We've been reinforced, hon. We need more ammunition."

"What will it be, Dino?" asked Aleck. "And don't tell me grog."

"I'm also a scotch man," he said to the waitress. "Neat."

Aleck asked, "Where is the dashing young hero?"

"I left Johnny at his father's house after the parade. I'm picking him up in a little while to take him to tonight's event at the junior high school."

"We can all go together in my car," said Scrappy.

"Thanks for the offer, but your very generous Buick dealer is providing a car and driver. I must say, the hospitality I've been shown by your town is overwhelming. I was expecting to stay in the bachelor officers' quarters at the Army hospital, but your mayor managed to get me a room in this hotel for free."

"It wasn't that hard to do," said Scrappy. "He owns the joint."

"Well, it's a hell of a lot better than a BOQ. What are the chances of me bumping into the ghost of General Washington in the hallway?"

"Slim," said Scrappy as the drinks were bought. "The place was built in 1892. It's on a spot that had a tavern and inn at the time Washington and his army camped at Valley

Forge, but I doubt that George paid it a visit. He made his headquarters in a comfortable stone house that still stands in Valley Forge Park. It's worthy of a visit. I'll be happy to take you on a tour."

"I may take you up on that."

"Enough of all this ancient history, Scrappy," exclaimed Aleck impatiently. "I'm more interested in hearing from the lieutenant about the young man he's been put in charge of."

Minetta took a sip of scotch. "What do you want to know?"

"To begin with, how does he feel about being suddenly thrust into the limelight?"

"He's thrilled and honored."

Aleck patted the officer's wrist. "Now, now, young man. The truth, please."

"I'm not kidding you. He's really thrilled and honored."

"Surely he must have expressed some uneasiness in coming back to a town which had so recently given him the heave-ho!"

"Does Johnny feel embarrassed by what happened? Yes, he does. I think I'm standing on firm ground by saying that he's repentant. On the day I met him in the hospital in Australia he asked to talk to a chaplain. But I don't believe it was because he needed to thank God for sparing his life."

"Interesting," said Scrappy. "Why do you think that?"

"I told him that the hospital had three chaplains—minister, priest, and rabbi. He said that for all that he'd done, he should probably see all of them. He finally talked to the priest. That was a surprise to me because I knew from looking at his service record that he's not Catholic."

"Perhaps he'd had a foxhole conversion."

"A lot of men in combat feel suddenly close to Jesus," Minetta said, "but usually when the shooting stops, so does the praying. My guess is that as he lay in that hospital bed thinking about nearly buying the farm with that bullet he took in the chest, he finally came to terms with his past, which evidently was not that of a kid who spent a lot of time in Sunday schools."

"Football was more his speed," said Scrappy. "And chasing girls, of course."

"He said he'd taken part in an armed robbery before the war."

"Indeed he did. But he wasn't the actual gunman."

"Yes, he told me he'd been a lookout. But I had a distinct feeling that it was weighing on his mind very heavily."

"Well, if he wants to lighten the burden," said Scrappy, "I'm sure our chief of police will be delighted to give him the opportunity. He's obsessed with that stickup."

"Why is that? I thought it was a closed case."

"One of the gang got away. Chief Detwiler believes Johnny knows where he is. Also, the loot was never found. The chief is convinced that it was stashed somewhere immediately after the robbery, and that Johnny Groover can take him to it."

"You said one of the gang got away. It stands to reason that he would have gotten the loot from wherever they'd hidden it—"

"And used it to finance his getaway," said Scrappy, nodding his head emphatically. "It's what I believe happened. But Chief Detwiler doesn't buy it. He believes the money is still here, and that Johnny Groover knows where it is. I expect that Detwiler will try to question him about it before Johnny slips through his hands again."

"Since Groover has paid the price for his deed, and in spades, I'd say," ventured Aleck in an indignant tone, "I fail to see how this policeman can expect to have any leverage whatever in the matter. Good lord, how can you arrest a man who is about to receive the Medal of Honor from FDR himself?"

Scrappy grunted. "Chief Detwiler is a Republican."

"The young man has already pleaded guilty," said Aleck. "Under the Constitution, which men are fighting around the world to preserve, Johnny Groover cannot be charged twice for the same offense!"

"Johnny pleaded guilty to taking part in the robbery," Scrappy replied. "But if he has lied about not knowing the whereabouts of Pete Slattery and the money, he can still be charged with aiding and abetting in a case of unlawful flight to avoid prosecution."

"You may be right," said Lieutenant Minetta, "but if it comes to that, because Groover is a Marine, your tenacious chief of police will first have to deal with me. And that means taking on the United States Navy."

Scrappy lifted his glass in a toast. "Damn the torpedoes, full speed ahead."

Aleck raised his scotch. "Remember Pearl Harbor!"

19

A FEW HOURS EARLIER there had been a disrupting scene in the hotel dining room. It began immediately after Patricia Roberts came in with a soldier. The reservation for an intimate corner table had been made by Corporal Robert Gordon, stationed at the Military Police Barracks at the George Washington Army Hospital.

The squabble started even before the couple's luncheon could be taken. In a voice that carried across the crowded room, he'd demanded, "You're still in love with Johnny Groover, aren't you?"

Hearing the name, people who had been at the parade stopped eating and talking to look at them in surprise and wonderment.

Looking around with an embarrassed expression, Pat whispered, "Bobby, please. People can hear you."

"Let 'em listen," he said angrily. "Answer me."

"If you don't lower your voice," she said patiently, "I'm leaving."

"Okay, okay," he said quietly as he raised his hands in surrender.

"How many times do I have to tell you that it's over between me and Johnny Groover? He knows it's over. I wrote him a letter telling him so."

"Then why did you insist on going to the train station to see him?"

"This is ludicrous. Half the people in town were at the station. It was a rare occasion. Robinsville's never had a war hero. Everybody wanted to see him."

"That's why you wore that red dress, isn't it? To be sure he'd notice you in the crowd."

"You're crazy."

"You wanted to stand out. You wore red so he'd be sure to spot you."

"If I were still in love with him, I wouldn't stand around in a crowd hoping he'd see me. And I certainly wouldn't have taken you along. If there was still something between Johnny and me, I would have been waiting for him at his house. It would be him I'd be having lunch with, not you. Really, Bobby, you've got to end this jealousy. It's gotten so that I can't even look at a boy I knew in school without you flying off the handle. I'm done with Johnny Groover. It's you I'm in love with. Now, can we please order lunch?"

"If I find out that you're seeing him again—"

"For crying out loud, he's only going to be here for a couple of days. Now, either you get off this subject, or you'll be having lunch by yourself."

"All right. But one more thing. I'm off duty on the night

of the big party that they're throwing for him at the junior high school gym, but you and I are not going to it. We're taking in the movie at the Colonial Theater."

"My sister plays clarinet in the high school swing band. Of course I'm going. Whether you go with me is entirely up to you."

"Go then," he snapped, pushing back his chair. "You can also have lunch alone!"

As he stormed from the dining room, all the eyes in the dining room fixed on her. Those of the men looked embarrassed and quickly turned away. The women's appeared outraged and sympathetic and lingered awhile. Not until she went outside did she let herself cry.

Lunch for Chief Tom Detwiler in his office at police headquarters was a zep sandwich from Brignola's on Main Street. It was made with three kinds of salami, half-moon slivers of provolone, sliced tomatoes, and thinly cut onions, layered on Italian bread and sprinkled with olive oil and finely diced oregano. Known as a hoagie in Philadelphia and its immediate environs, and called a submarine in most other places on the East Coast, the Robinsville version had been named a zeppelin. At some point in time, for a reason long since lost in local history, this was shortened to zep. If someone wanted one that was tangier, it could be topped with slices of hot peppers. Although the chief of police enjoyed the peppers, they left him suffering excruciating bouts of heartburn. Therefore, Theresa Brignola had a standing order not to add them, even if requested. She also knew that the zep was to be cut into thirds, rather than in customary halves.

Joining Chief Detwiler for lunch was Officer Todd Doebling. His meal was a steak and cooked sliced-onion sandwich served on a zep roll that became a soggy, drippy handful. Pausing to wipe his greasy mouth more than halfway through the long sandwich, he ventured, "Everything went very well this morning, don't you think, Chief? It was a much bigger turnout than I expected."

Barely into the first third of the zep, Detwiler said, "That's because they let the kids off from school." He paused to sip Coca-Cola. "And who doesn't like a parade, even if it is for a bum who rightfully belongs in prison?"

Doebling's drink was Pepsi, which everyone knew from a singing commercial on the radio came in a much taller and fatter bottle than the squat, hour-glass-shaped Coke. "Pepsi-Cola hits the spot," the ditty went. "Twelve full ounces, that's a lot. Twice as much for nickel, too. Pepsi-Cola is the drink for you." But anyone who liked to spike a glass of rum with a cola also knew that the best one for that purpose was Coke. And people who had never even thought of having a highball had learned about "drinkin' rum and Coca-Cola" from the hit record by the Andrews Sisters.

Thinking about these songs as he devoured his steak sandwich, Doebling asked the chief of police, "I'll bet you that it won't be long before someone writes a song about the Groover kid and how heroic he was at Guadalcanal. That's what they did for some guy named Roger Young, on account of his actions on the island of New Georgia in the Solomons. The song 'Comin' in on a Wing and a Prayer' was also a true story."

Detwiler paused in picking up the second third of the zep. "Propaganda."

"Wait a minute. Are you telling me those songs aren't true?"

"They're true, but they're embellished. Right now the country's crazy over heroes, but once the people wake up to the fact that thousands of men won't be coming home, the reality of this war is going to hit home. And hit hard. In the meantime you and I have the unpleasant task of keeping order while laurels are heaped on an accomplice in a still-unsolved crime."

"I know you're upset about Groover getting let off from doing jail time," said Doebling, "but the crime he took part in *was* solved. And in very short order, I point out. Thanks to you, two of the crooks are doing hard time and one of them is in a reformatory until he's twenty-one."

"And I point out to you," Detwiler retorted, "that the whereabouts of Pete Slattery aren't known, and neither is what happened to the money. Until I have the answers to those questions, the payroll robbery stays open on our books. I also promise you that before Sergeant Groover leaves town again, he's going to be talked to. I don't give a damn if he is the hero of the entire country. Or how many baloney songs get written about him. Or if FDR and Eleanor Roosevelt kiss him on the lips, or the ass, when he gets the Congressional Medal of Honor. That bastard is going to come clean on that payroll stickup even if I have to beat it out of him."

At the Vale-Rio Diner a star-spangled paper banner had been stretched across the wall behind the counter. The special on a small white card with a red border was clipped to the regular menu. Typed in blue was IN HONOR OF SERGEANT JOHNNY GROOVER: OUR ALL-AMERICAN

LUNCH. For fifty cents a customer got a hamburger with the bun spiked by a tiny paper U.S. flag on a toothpick, home-fried potatoes, cole slaw, a wedge of blueberry pie with a scoop each of strawberry and vanilla ice cream, and a mug of coffee (one sugar only, owing to the shortage).

The song on the jukebox as both Coach Franklin and Richie Zale ordered the special was "I'll Be Seeing You," by Frank Sinatra with Tommy Dorsey and his orchestra.

"Because we haven't talked for so long," said Franklin, "lunch is on me. No argument!"

"Thanks. But next time, I pay."

"How have you been, Richie? How's the missus? And the kids?"

"They're all fine. So am I, even though I've been working my balls off at the steel plant. I've been catching quite a few double shifts, on account of the manpower shortage."

"I was disappointed that you couldn't go to college."

Richie shrugged. "I probably would have been drafted out of school anyway. Now I'm in a job that the government calls 'essential to the war effort,' so I wouldn't be accepted in the service if I volunteered."

"Someone's got to turn out the steel for the ships and tanks."

As the record in the jukebox changed to "Till Then" by the Mills Brothers, a waitress brought the hamburger platters.

When she set down the coffees, Richie asked, "Could I have a Coke instead?"

"It'll be extra."

"That's fine," Franklin interjected. "Bring him a large."

Plucking the flag from the bun, Richie said, "I saw a

couple of the Phantoms' games last year. I couldn't get to all because I was working. You had a good season."

"There will never be another Batman and Robin," said the coach, removing the flag. "It must have been great for you seeing Johnny again."

"Yeah, it was. Of course, we didn't have a lot of time to talk."

"In spite of everything he's been through physically, I thought he looked well. He could probably get into his old football uniform with no problem. I've still got it if he'd like to try it on. Yours, too. I keep them in a locker at the field house. I don't know if you noticed when you were at the games last season, but I retired both your numbers. Seven and eleven."

"They sure were lucky ones."

The coach reached across the table and squeezed Richie's right bicep. "Nonsense. Luck had nothing to do with it. You boys were *talented*." Letting go of the arm, he smiled. "You've obviously kept as fit as a fiddle."

"It's the job," Richie replied, biting into the burger. "Working in a steel plant keeps me in pretty good shape."

"That must keep the missus happy."

Chewing, Richie replied, "No complaints so far."

"I imagine Johnny will find himself fighting the girls off while he's at home."

"There's nothing new about that. He's always been good at getting laid."

Franklin chuckled. "He wasn't always the expert swordsman. I remember shortly after he went out for football when he came to see me, very worried, because he'd gotten laid for the first time and wasn't sure if he'd used the rubber properly." Laughing now, he continued, "It was an old one that he'd pilfered from his father's bureau drawer. He was so terribly naive that I was surprised he even knew about prophylactics."

Richie shook his head. "He certainly didn't learn of them in your boys' hygiene class."

"Teaching about sex was forbidden, of course. It still is. Stupid!"

"You sure could have cleared up a lot of misinformation," said Richie as the Coca-Cola arrived. He waited until the waitress was out of earshot. "How old was Johnny when he asked you about rubbers?"

"He was in the ninth grade. That would make him fifteen?"

Shaking his head, Richie said, "That bastard! Laid at fifteen! Hell, I didn't get my first piece of tail till I was seventeen." Looking around the crowded diner, he continued in a whisper. "Did Johnny tell you who the girl was that he had when he was fifteen?"

"He did, but I've forgotten her name. Not that I'd tell anyone if I remembered it."

"I'm sorry if I put you on the spot."

"You didn't. However, I'm surprised you didn't know. I was led to believe there were no secrets between Batman and Robin," said Franklin as Richie sipped the soda. "Will there be another reunion of you and Johnny at the reception this evening?"

"I have to work four to twelve tonight."

"I'm sure Johnny will be disappointed. Me, too. It could be like the old times again."

"That was then, Coach. This is now. Johnny and I aren't kids anymore."

"I know what we can do! Suppose I invite Johnny to my

place after tonight's big to-do? You can come around when you get off work at midnight."

"It would be nice to see him without a huge crowd around him."

Afternoons of
Grace and Glory

"GROOVER AND ZALE. Seven and eleven. What a combination," said Scrappy MacFarland as he got up again and headed to the bathroom. "I never saw anybody like them, before and since."

He went into the bathroom carrying the stub of his cigar. When he emerged without it, I regretted that I had brought him only two.

"When those boys took to the field," he continued, resuming his chair, "you knew that you were in for an exciting afternoon. And even if the Phantoms wound up losing, you left the grandstand having witnessed a glorious display of grace."

"I guess they were natural-born athletes."

"Native ability is necessary, sure. But to fashion it into victory on the gridiron you must understand that there's more to the game than muscle. You have to use your mind.

And you can only learn how to *think football* from a great coach."

"Okay. Johnny Groover owed his success on the football field to the coaching of Ralph Franklin, but—forgive me for sounding impatient—I don't see what that has to do with my reason for being here, which is to find out about Johnny's death."

"Winning at football requires teamwork."

"I'm sorry, I don't follow."

He sighed in exasperation. "All the boys who took part in that robbery had at one time or another played football, except for the youngest of the Perillo kids. Rico hadn't been old enough to go out for the team. Football was the only thing those boys had in common."

"Okay. But what's your point?"

"There are two points, actually. The first is that they pulled off that robbery as slickly as a well-executed football play. The second is that the only one of them who was smart enough to plan it was Johnny Groover."

"Wait a minute! The police theory at the time was that the mastermind was Sal Perillo."

"That idea was pure baloney. Sal is as bright as a fence post."

"He didn't deny it."

"Put yourself in his place. The police have you dead to rights and are saying that you're a criminal mastermind. For the first time in your life, instead of being called a dim bulb, you are credited with being a genius. The stupid jerk was too damn flattered to deny that he planned it."

"It's your belief the holdup was Johnny's idea?"

"I think the idea of robbing the payroll came from Pete

Slattery. Johnny figured out how to do it most efficiently. I'm certain he was the coach who designed the play."

"But everyone involved said he was just a lookout."

"You're a smart fellow. If you were planning a caper in which a gun was being used and in which it was possible that the muscle men who would be closest to the action might get shot, where would you station yourself?"

"Why would a basically good kid, the star of the football team and heartthrob of all the girls in school, get involved in such a scheme?"

"For the sheer thrill? For one-fifth of the big haul? To prove that he could do it? Who can tell? What prompted him to perform acts of heroism on Guadalcanal?"

"Didn't you ever ask him?"

"Everyone asked him. When I put the question to him in the town jail a few hours after Detwiler and Doebling collared him at the field house, he just grinned at me like the Cheshire cat that ate the canary. He was just a kid and kids are capable of doing really dumb things."

"How did the police know where to look for him?"

"They went after him just before suppertime, expecting to pick him up at his house. When they asked poor Harry Groover where they would be likely to find him, the old man had no idea what was going on. When he asked the cops why they were looking for his son, Detwiler gave him a cock-and-bull story about the kid having been a witness to a traffic accident. Mr. Groover told them he often went running on the track around the football field."

"Back up a minute," I said. "How did the police know to go looking for Johnny and the rest of the gang?"

"They got a tip. Phoned in. Male voice. Anonymous, of

course. But I think the call was probably made by Pete Slattery. On his way out of town. With the fifty grand."

"The old double cross."

"A typical Pete Slattery move."

"Whatever possessed Johnny to get involved with him?"

"I guess you could call it idol worship. When Johnny first went out for football, Pete was a senior and the greatest player the Phantoms ever had, until Johnny showed his stuff. Did you see the movie a few years ago with the Dead End Kids as a gang that looked up to the gangster that was played by Jimmy Cagney?"

"Angels with Dirty Faces."

"Think of Pete Slattery as Cagney. The difference between the two is that at the end of the movie, Cagney's character did a noble thing by pretending he was afraid to go to the chair, so that the gang would read in the newspapers that the hero they'd worshiped was a coward."

"Didn't it come to Johnny's mind that the reason Slattery skipped out was that Slattery had betrayed them?"

"It's pretty difficult for anybody to accept that his idol has clay feet. It's even harder if you're seventeen years old."

"You're very forgiving."

"The older you get, forgiving comes easier. I'm so old now that I can't think of anyone I haven't forgiven from that time. Except Hitler. And the sons of bitches who thought they could get away with a sneak attack on Pearl Harbor."

"I think you were able to forgive Johnny Groover because deep down you liked him. In your mind you don't see a kid who planned the biggest robbery in this town's history, or even the hero of Guadalcanal. The Johnny Groover you see is the kid who showed you grace and glory on crisp, autumn afternoons on a football field."

"There's an old saying in journalism that can serve you well, young man, when you sit down at your typewriter in the city room of the *Independence*—excuse me, your computer! It goes, 'When you don't know what's truth and what's legend, print the legend.'"

20

"**H**OW COME YOU'RE not wearing the fancy outfit?" asked Harry Groover as he stood in the doorway of the tiny bedroom above the kitchen watching his son put on Marine Corps greens. "I thought you looked really sharp in that blue uniform."

"It's too dressy for tonight," said Johnny, "Blues are for ceremonies and parades. If it was up to me, I'd put on civvies. But Lieutenant Minetta says I have to wear class A's."

"Who's Lieutenant Minetta?"

"He's the Naval officer assigned to hold my hand during all this bullshit. You would have met him if you'd been at the station. He's picking me up in a little while with a car to take me to the big event tonight. He says people will be expecting to see me in uniform."

"Being in the Marines doesn't seem to have changed you at all. You look the same as the day you went away."

"*Sent away,* you mean. Yeah, I'm the same guy, except for a couple of scars."

"Did you really kill that many Japs? The stories in the paper said you got two hundred."

"I didn't stop to count 'em, Pop. They kept coming. I kept shooting."

"When I read about it, I thought someone probably made up the number."

Standing before a mirror, Johnny assessed his appearance. Satisfied, he turned to face his father and was shocked at how much older he seemed to have become. His brown hair had more gray in it and he appeared to have lost a lot of weight. The white shirt he always wore seemed a size too big. Green work pants looked baggy on him. A tightly drawn black belt pulled the cloth into bunches at the waist.

Stepping away from the mirror, Johnny said, "I really don't want to talk about the war."

"I've kept all the letters that you wrote me."

Moving toward the door, Johnny asked, "What the hell for?"

"On account of I didn't know if I'd ever see you again."

"Well, now you have," said Johnny as his father stepped aside to let him pass, "so burn the damn things."

"You didn't write me very often anyway."

Johnny started down the steps. "I wrote when I could."

"In spite of what happened before you went away," said Harry, following him slowly, "people asked me about you all the time."

"Yeah, I'll bet."

"It's true. Your football coach always wanted to know how you were doing and where you were. Judge Wooten asked me, too. And a couple of your old girlfriends. The one named Roberts used to inquire a lot, but hasn't lately."

Johnny grunted. "She sent me a letter saying she's got a new boyfriend."

"And the pretty one that married the Zale boy asked about you," said Harry as they reached the bottom of the stairs. "They have two kids now, boy and girl."

"I saw Richie and Coach Franklin at the station. They were up on the stage. The chief of police was there, too, with the cop who was with him when he arrested me at the field house. He stared daggers at me all through the ceremonies."

"Detwiler comes around every now and then."

"What the hell for?"

"He seems to think that I know what happened to the money."

"What a jerk," said Johnny, going into the parlor. "You should get yourself a lawyer to tell Detwiler to lay off you. No. I'll tell him myself when I see him tonight at the gym."

"Don't go stirring things up, Johnny. It doesn't bother me that he comes around."

Johnny drew aside a lace curtain and peered through the window. "Well, it pisses me off. I've paid for what I did, so he should leave you the hell alone."

"It's the man's nature. As long as I've known him, he's been bullheaded. I suppose that's why he became a cop. And do you know who always asks me about you? Tommy Fallon's oldest girl."

Johnny dropped onto the couch. "Kate asks about me? That's odd. I hardly knew her. She was a couple of years ahead of me in school."

"I see her sometimes when I'm delivering milk to her house and she's on the way out to work. She's got a job as a welder at Manyon's."

"Kate's a *welder*?"

"A lot of women are doing men's work on account of the shortage of manpower."

"Scrappy MacFarland told me that Kate and Mrs. Bradshaw from the bookstore are in charge of arranging all these ceremonies."

"The mayor gave them the job of setting up the town's servicemen's center, so they were the logical choices for it, I guess."

The sound of a car pulling up in front of the house caused Johnny to turn and look out the window. A moment later, Lieutenant Minetta got out on the passenger side of a Buick sedan.

"Here's my baby-sitter," said Johnny.

"Have yourself a swell time, my boy."

"I don't know why you insist on staying home tonight, Pop."

"You know me. Early to bed and early to rise, else the milk doesn't get delivered."

"For once in your life, Pop," said Johnny as the doorbell rang, "screw the milk."

"If I went to this shindig," Harry replied as they went to the door, "I'd only embarrass you by falling asleep right in the middle of it."

When Johnny opened the door, Minetta grinned. "Ready for your big night?"

"Lieutenant," said Johnny. "Meet my father."

"Glad to meet you, Mr. Groover," said Minetta, touching the black visor of his white hat. "You must be very proud of your boy. Johnny says you won't be attending the evening's affair. I'm sorry to hear that."

"I'm feeling a little under the weather, but I'm sure Johnny will be in good hands. And what young fella wants his old man hanging around when he's having a good time, right?"

Minetta asked Johnny, "Where's your cane?"

"The hell with it. That damn stick makes me feel like I'm a bigger freak than I am."

21

STANDING BY HIS five-year-old Plymouth sedan parked in front of the General Washington Hotel, Scrappy said to Aleck, "We've got a little time before we're due at the junior high school. How about I take you for a spin around town?"

"Excellent! If it's not out of the way, I'd also like to have a look at the scene of Johnny Groover's stickup caper. In reconstructing a crime for my listeners, I'll be able to give them a feel for the lay of the land."

"It's not *in* town, but sure, we can take a swing out to Coldstream Road," said Scrappy as he went around the car to the driver's side. "But there's not much to see, especially at night."

Settled into the passenger's seat, Aleck asked, "The holdup was in broad daylight?"

"It happened around two-thirty in the afternoon. The payroll was to be delivered to the steel plant at three, so the pay would be ready for men reporting for the four o'clock shift, and the ones getting off from work."

"They were all paid in cash?"

"Not too many of the employees have bank accounts. In most cases, when the man gets home, he hands over the money to the wife," said Scrappy, starting the car. "Business in a town like this is conducted on a cash-and-carry basis. It's the women who do the shopping."

"I have a banker friend in New York who believes that in the future all financial transactions will be done on the basis of credit," Aleck said as they drove away. "The system will employ an encoded card similar to those used in a few of the large department stores. Rather than carry wads of cash, a shopper presents the card. At the end of the month a bill is sent, which is then paid by mailing back a check. My friend insists that the time is not far in the offing when we will be what he calls a cashless society."

"I don't think the guy at the Esso station who pumps gas into this rattle trap of a car will be much interested in sending me a bill every month when he's getting cash on the barrelhead, so to speak."

"According to my banker, your bill will come from the company that issues your card."

"How does my gas station owner get his dough?"

"He's paid by the card issuer."

The car proceeded slowly through an area of stores, restaurants, and many shoppers on the pavements. The marquee of a movie theater had the name *Colonial* in huge, yellow neon letters. The title of the feature attraction was in black letters on a white, illuminated background. *Journey for Margaret* was a story about a wartime migrant, played by five-year-old Margaret O'Brien, herself a refugee from England. A reporter, portrayed by Robert Young, and his wife, Laraine Day, rescued Margaret and other orphans. Commenting on the film on his program, Aleck had told his radio audience, "There is pain in this film. It is a hurt that will remain long after these desperate years and all the children of a world in which bombs fall have learned to trust the sky—and more, to trust human beings. It is going to take more than victory alone to dry the tears of the Margarets of this world. But the compassion in this movie will go far to help."

Passing The Book Nook, Scrappy said, "You and Bea Bradshaw seem to have hit it off."

"She's a grand lady of the old school," said Aleck.

Scrappy turned from Bridge Street onto Main. "Ahead on the left is the police station."

Aleck peered at a two-story, gray stone structure with fluted pillars flanking double glass doors. Above them was a green sign with POLICE in painted gold letters. "It looks like a bank."

"That's what it was before the Depression," Scrappy replied. "After FDR closed all the banks in 1933, it never reopened. I'm happy to say that my money, and I had very little of it back then, was in the Farmer's and Mechanics Savings and Loan, which managed to survive the crisis. The police department at that time was two offices and one jail cell in the basement of the Town Hall."

With the police station behind them, Aleck chuckled as he asked, "What did the coppers do with the overflow?"

"If the cell was insufficient, the arrestees, if there's such a word, were taken over to the county lockup in West

Chester. The new police station has seven cells in the basement."

"How large is the force?"

"In addition to Chief Detwiler there's a sergeant, Bill Hargreave, who's on an emergency leave at the moment to spend time with a sister in Philly who just learned that her husband was killed in New Guinea. And there are four officers. One of them is a plainclothes detective, name of Todd Doebling."

"As I recall, he's the one who arrested Johnny Groover!"

"Chief Detwiler actually placed Johnny under arrest. Doebling handcuffed him. I'll take you past the spot where it happened, if you're interested."

"I certainly am."

"It happened in the football team's locker room at Washington Field."

"Is *everything* in this town named after old George?"

Five minutes later, Scrappy parked the car at a gate in a wire fence that surrounded the football field. To the left of the gridiron was a stretch of bleachers. To the right was a roofed, wooden grandstand. Beyond this stood a low cinder-block building with a flat roof.

"Again, it's not much to see," said Scrappy. "The bleachers used to be smaller, but they were extended two years ago to accommodate bigger crowds at the games. They were built after Johnny Groover's final season. As a matter of fact, they were under construction at the time he was arrested. The covered building is pretty old. It was put up around the turn of the century when there was a racetrack on this site. It went the way of all flesh in the twenties when the town clergymen who viewed horse racing as a sin raised holy hell about it. They also did their best to shut down the speakeasies, but with less success."

"And the cement building next to it that looks like a bunker on the Maginot Line?"

"That's the field house where Johnny was taken into custody. When Chief Detwiler and Officer Doebling arrived, they found him in the office of the football coach, Ralph Franklin. You met him at the ceremony at the train station."

"Have you noticed that all football coaches look like Pat O'Brien in that Ronald Reagan movie about football at Notre Dame?"

"To the people of Robinsville," said Scrappy, "Coach Franklin is as revered as Knute Rockne is in South Bend, Indiana. That's what comes with producing championship teams. It's the American way. We hate to lose, so we love people who refuse to give up, even if they do lose in the end. You saw that in the soldiers who held out at Corregidor. The people of this town also saw it in Johnny Groover when he took over that machine gun in the face of what appeared to be an overwhelming number of Japs. He could have turned tail and run. But he stayed put and never let go of the trigger until all the ammo was gone. For that, this town has forgiven him for what he did on Coldstream Road. Which, if you've seen enough here, is where we will now go."

"Yes, please. I would like to see it."

When they arrived at the point in a valley of the winding country road two-and-a-half miles out of town, Scrappy parked at the place where Delmer Turner had stopped his truck to go to the aid of a boy who'd fallen off his bicycle. The car's headlights that illuminated the spot also glistened on patches of snow between winter-bare bushes and in the thickets of leafless trees on both sides of the blacktop roadway.

"It was summertime then, of course," said Scrappy as he lit a cigar, "so the driver of the truck wasn't able to see the figures in the foliage."

"Where was Johnny Groover at the time?"

Scrappy pointed forward. "He was at the top of that rise, watching for any vehicle that might come from that direction. The other lookout, the youngest of the Perillo brothers, kept a lookout on the hill we just came down."

"Which of them was the kid with the bicycle?"

"That was Dominic Perillo. Sal and Pete Slattery were the ones in the bushes. It was over in under a minute. Turner was so scared, he wasn't able to tell the cops anything more than that he'd been held up by a gang. Chief Detwiler immediately assumed Turner had been in on it, of course. He remained under suspicion until the cops got the anonymous tip that put them on to the Perillos and Johnny. They implicated Pete Slattery. By then, he was long gone."

"Of course he was. He made the phone call. He played those kids for saps."

"Wherever Pete is," said Scrappy, putting the car in gear, "I wonder if he knows that one of the kids he took for a sap is now the man of the hour?"

22

POKING HIS HEAD into the back bedroom on the second floor of a large, graceful white house on Pennsylvania Avenue, Paulie Fallon found his sister Kate standing before her dressing table. Wearing a plain black dress, she gazed into the mirror as she put on a string of pearls that Mike had given to her two Christmases ago. Seeing his reflection, she asked, "How do I look?"

Paulie shrugged. "You look good."

"Mrs. Bee says you can't go wrong with basic black."

The last time she'd worn the dress, she remembered, was to Amanda Burford Griffith's funeral. She'd bought the dress a year before that sad occasion for the funerals of Nancy Edinger and John Bohannon. All had been murdered. Mrs. Griffith was killed in her home by her maid. In a frenzy of resentment and jealousy the poor, demented woman had also slain other members of the Molly Pitcher Society. Nancy Edinger had died at the hands of a jealous member of the town's police force, who had then killed Mr. Bohanon out of fear of being exposed.

By a twist of fate and circumstance, Kate remembered with a shudder, she had helped to solve the murders in both cases.

Shaking off the ugly memories, she turned around to face her brother and asked, "Do you think these pearls are too dressy?"

Paulie took a hesitant step into the room. "How should I know? They look nice."

From the foot of the stairs came their mother's voice. "Paulie, your supper's on the table. Don't make me have to call you again."

"You're not eating?" Paulie asked as Kate turned to the mirror.

"I'm too nervous about tonight to even think of food. If I get hungry later, there will be plenty of it available at the reception."

"With all the fuss everybody's making over Johnny Groover," said Paulie, "you'd think that he'd gone and won the war all by himself. All he did was kill a bunch of Japs, which is what a Marine is supposed to do."

"Two hundred men killed is more than a bunch. You're just making it sound like nothing because you're not allowed to go to the reception."

Paulie smiled. "Mom would let me go if you asked her to."

"This evening is not for children. It will probably last till eleven o'clock, or even later, and you have school tomorrow. Now leave me be and go to supper."

As her brother thumped down the stairs, she looked at the bedside clock and decided she had enough time to start a letter to Mike before Beatrice Bradshaw came around to pick her up in her car. Seated at the dresser, she took out a sheet of pale blue stationery and wrote:

My darling,

It's the night of the reception for Johnny Groover and I'm sitting in my bedroom waiting for Mrs. Bee to "collect me," as she put it in her English way of speaking. I'm as nervous as a turkey before Thanksgiving Day! So far, everything has gone very well. There was a huge crowd for the welcoming ceremony at the train station yesterday, followed by a big parade up Bridge Street. The only cloud in the sky is Chief Detwiler. He can't seem to get over the fact that all this "fuss," as Paulie sees it, is for a kid whom the chief would prefer to be locked up in jail for a few years because of his role in the payroll robbery. I think it really grated on him, and on Officer Doebling, that everyone in town is willing to forgive and forget. All through the ceremony at the station they glared at Johnny as if he was Jack the Ripper.

I'm also feeling nervous because the famous radio personality, Alexander Whiteside, has come to town to take part in all the events to honor Johnny. He's an old friend of Scrappy's from their newspaper days in New York. He is also a close friend of President Roosevelt. But what bothers me is that he says he wants to do a radio program about ME. He believes I'm some kind of master sleuth because of my involvement in solving the recent murders. I place the blame for this belief on Scrappy. But Aleck—that's what he insists I call him—is a very nice person who seems to know everyone of any importance in the world. Mrs. Bee has been smitten by him. I'm doing everything I can think of to talk Aleck out of this crazy idea of talking about me on his program, but he seems to be quite hard-headed on the subject.

As to Johnny Groover, I found him to be surprisingly shy about his sudden role as war hero. Except for a cane, he seems mostly recovered from his wounds. Accompanying him is a very nice Naval officer named Dino Minetta. He was so handsome in his white dress uniform that if I weren't madly in love with a guy in khakis, I could easily fall for him.

Johnny looked neat in his formal uniform, too. I could see from the speaker's platform that most of the girls in the crowd couldn't take their eyes off him for a second. I noticed that a few of them were girls that he dated in school, including Pat Roberts, who seems to have gotten a new boyfriend. He was in an Army uniform and had his arm around her the entire time, very possessively.

Coach Franklin was there, too, up on the speaker's platform, along with Richie Zale. The coach insisted on calling them by their old football nicknames, Batman and Robin, which seemed to embarrass both of them.

Mayor Cantrell made his usual pompous speech, but Scrappy was funny in his brief remarks. Aleck wasn't called on to address the crowd because he'll be offering remarks tonight and later in the week when the mayor presents Johnny with the key to the town.

At the sound of a car horn, Kate hurriedly wrote:

There's Mrs. Bee, come to collect me. I'll finish this letter after I get home from tonight's festivities, or if I'm too tired to do anything but tumble into bed, tomorrow.

Her mother yelled up the stairs, "Katie, Mrs. Bee's car is out front!"

Checking her appearance in the mirror and deciding the pearls were not too dressy, Kate shouted, "Coming right down, Mom."

In Patricia Roberts's bedroom the attire chosen was the red dress she had worn to the railway station, obviously to the chagrin of Bobby Gordon. She could still hear the anger and jealousy in his voice during lunch at the General Washington Hotel.

"You're still in love with Johnny Groover, aren't you?"

Utter nonsense. She'd sent him a Dear John letter. It was over between them.

"That's why you wore that red dress, isn't it?"

A ridiculous accusation!

"So he would be sure to notice you in the crowd. You wanted to stand out. You wore red so he'd be sure to spot you."

There must have been a thousand people there.

"If I find out that you're seeing him again—"

What fools men could be!

• • •

In the bedroom of Chief of Police Tom Detwiler, his wife expressed surprise to find him putting on his every-day uniform. "At the train station you wore your formal outfit," she said, "so how come you're not dressing up for tonight?"

"The train station was an official ceremony. Tonight's a *casual reception,* as that woman from the bookstore went out of her way to phone me at headquarters this afternoon and remind me in that irritating, uppity tone of hers."

"Beatrice Bradshaw is not uppity. She's English."

"The woman has lived in this town for more than twenty years. She could have lost that limey accent if she'd really wanted to."

"It's not her way of talking that's got you in a snit."

"I am not in a snit."

"You're miffed that you have to take part in honoring the Groover boy."

"You're damn right I'm miffed."

"If this affair tonight is casual, and going to it is just going to upset you, don't go."

"I'm going in my official capacity. I intend to inform that smug son of a bitch that before he leaves town, he's to come down to headquarters for an official interview. He can come in on his own, or he can be brought in by Officer Doebling."

"Now you listen to me, Thomas Detwiler," she said, wagging a finger under his nose. "I don't want you making a fool of yourself and embarrassing me in front of the whole town by causing a scene at tonight's affair."

"I intend to do my duty. If you're afraid that will embarrass you, you can stay home."

"Very well, I'll do just that."

"Fine!"

In the parlor of the Zack house, Millie had finally stopped crying.

At a quarter to four Richie had stormed out to go to work at the steel plant. Asked by Millie as he left what time she should expect him to come home, he'd snapped. "I'll be home when I get here."

"I don't want you hanging out in a bar and drinking until closing time, and then coming in drunk and waking up the kids."

Showered, shaved, and with only a dash of Vitalis to keep his short brown hair looking neat, Ralph Franklin stood naked in front of a long mirror on the back of the bathroom door. He was pleased with the tone of his physique, the result of his morning runs and three-times-a-week, hour-long workout with barbells and weights in the locker room at the field house. His weight when he'd gotten on the scale that morning registered only ten pounds more than when he had played football in college.

Going to his bedroom, he took out of his closet the gray double-breasted suit he'd had cleaned and pressed for the occasion. To go with it he selected a tie with diagonal purple and white stripes, the colors of the Robinsville Phantoms.

Delmer Turner had spent the day hemming and hawing in his head about whether to go into town and pay the cost of a War Bond to get into the disgraceful event at the junior high school gym. If he did so, he could look into the eyes of Johnny Groover and in so doing let him know just by staring at him how much he hated him for ruining the life of the man that he'd helped rob, not only of the steel company's money, but a hardworking and honest man of his reputation and self-respect.

23

ENTERING THE GYMNASIUM of Memorial Junior High School half an hour before the doors were to be opened to the public, Scrappy and Aleck were greeted by Kate and Beatrice.

Wearing a becoming plain black cocktail dress with a rope of pearls and beaming with pride, Kate said, "It's supposed to be Rick's *Café Americain* in the movie *Casablanca*."

Aleck gazed in wonder and admiration at white-painted cardboard arches placed against walls that were dotted with gaudy travel posters of prewar North African locales, a scattering of potted plants, four palm trees with trunks fabricated from large mailing tubes and leaves made of green crepe paper, and a dance floor bordered by a dozen round tables with white covers and flickering candles in votive cups. Of this clever evocation of the nightclub in the film the portly radio celebrity patted his ample belly and through a rumbling laugh exclaimed, "I feel just like Sidney Greenstreet, but without the fez."

"Even though Johnny Groover was at Guadalcanal," Kate said, "we couldn't very well turn the gym into a jungle, could we? Then a few days ago when I was leaving my job at Manyon's Precision Metals, a coworker got to talking about the movie and how romantic and exotic it was. I thought it would be fun to decorate the gym like Rick's. I was reluctant at first because my fiancé happens to be serving in North Africa. I didn't want people to get the idea that I was somehow paying tribute to him. When I discussed the idea with Mrs. Bee, she loved it. And that was that."

"It's a wonderful idea, my dear," said Aleck. "I've been to the French North Africa, so I know whereof I speak. I was there just after the First World War. I'd been in France working for the newspaper *Stars and Stripes.* In May of 1919 I was on a transport that sailed from Marseilles. We stopped in Oran for coal and were delayed in port for five days by a longshoremen's strike. I spent most of my time cavorting on the waters of the gulf of Mers el Kebir. I rented a terribly becoming one-piece bathing suit with wide alternate stripes of shell pink and baby blue."

"I've got one word of advice for you, Kate," said Scrappy. "If you've got gambling in the back room, take a cue from Rick Blaine and let the chief of police win. Otherwise, Detwiler will blow his whistle, order everyone out, and close the place down."

"The only element missing," said Beatrice, "is the colored piano player to sing 'As Time Goes By.' The music will be provided by the senior high school jazz band."

"They spent the afternoon rehearsing," said Kate. "They're really very good."

"I'm looking forward to dancing with you and Beatrice," Aleck said, "so I hope the band plays something slow now and then. I'm too old and fat for jitterbugging."

"That's not what I read in a Winchell column recently," said Scrappy. "Walter wrote that you were seen in one of those hot nightspots on Forty-second Street. The item said that you were cutting a mean rug with Judy Garland to the tune of 'The Jersey Bounce.'"

"That was a triple lie. It wasn't in one of those Swing Street dives, it was the Roseland Ballroom. The song was 'Jumpin' Punkins.' And my partner was Ethel Merman."

Beatrice exclaimed, "Is there any famous person that you don't know?"

Aleck thought for a moment. "There is one," he declared. "The High Lama of Tibet. He lives too far away, and he *never* comes to New York."

"Of all the celebrities you know or have known," said Kate, "which have you found most interesting? No, let me put it this way. If there was one person you could have dinner with—anyone in the whole wide world—this evening, who would you choose?"

"Why you, of course."

"Come on," said Kate, blushing a little, "no kidding."

"I'm serious. Before I leave your charming town, I intend to interview you on the subject of your remarkable ability to solve baffling crimes."

"I can tell you in two words," said Kate. "Dumb luck. Now give me a serious answer to my question. Of all the people in the world, past or present, who would you like to invite to have dinner with you this evening?"

"I'd pick the world's most famous vegetarian, Herr Hitler himself," said Aleck, "so I could douse his sauerkraut with poison."

"Other than Hitler. Someone whose meal you wouldn't wish to poison."

"Given that limitation, I'd invite Jesus Christ."

"Assuming your invitation were accepted," Scrappy interjected, "what would be the most important, the most burning subject on your mind?"

With a mischievous smile, Aleck replied, "What to serve for the *entrée*."

As the women giggled, Scrappy said, "Ladies, I think that's Aleck's method of asking to be pointed to the buffet table."

"Right this way," said Beatrice gaily as she entwined arms with Aleck. "Because of shortages of meats, I'm sorry to say that the fare must be limited. I do hope you like a seafood salad. There is also a selection of pasta dishes. And plenty of vegetables."

As Aleck and the others made their way to the buffet, the members of the six-piece band began warming up with an initially squeaky rendition of "Skylark." With a gentle tap of his hand to Beatrice's shoulder, Scrappy said, "Whatcha say, toots? Care to cut a rug?"

As they danced, Aleck surveyed the offerings of the long buffet table. "I suppose it's too much to ask that band to stick to Hoagy Carmichael songs all evening," he said to Kate while he heaped a plate with a sample of each dish. "Some Cole Porter and Duke Ellington would also be nice." Noticing that Kate had not taken a plate, he exclaimed, "Good heavens, darling, aren't you going to have *anything*?"

"I'm too keyed up and nervous to eat."

"You've got nothing to fret about, my dear," he said as they went to a table for four. "The evening's going to be a five-star smash hit."

Looking anxiously at a slender gold wristwatch, she said, "The doors open in a couple of minutes. I had a dream the other night that nobody showed up."

"You're offering them food, drink, music, and a hometown-born war hero, my darling. In spite of the fifty-dollar War Bond admission, you won't be able to squeeze them all in."

"Oh, don't say that! It never occurred to me that the gym might be too small."

The music changed to the brassy "Boogie Woogie Bugle Boy."

Turning toward the dance floor expecting to find Beatrice and Scrappy leaving it, Kate smiled at the sight of them doing their best to do the jitterbug.

With a groan, Aleck said, "I shall never forgive the Andrews Sisters for recording that song! You hear it everywhere. It's impossible to escape."

Turning her eyes from the dancers to him, Kate said, "That's what happens when a song makes it onto the Hit Parade."

"I don't believe it was dumb luck."

"No. I'm sure a lot of hard work is required to turn a song into a hit."

"I was referring to your successes in solving murders."

"You mustn't take what Scrappy tells you as gospel truth. He has a way of embroidering tales. Oh! That sounded awful. I wasn't saying that he embroiders stories in his newspaper."

Ignoring his food, Aleck said, "When I told him I intended to talk to you about the two murder cases for a broadcast, he warned me that you'd play down your role in solving them."

"I find it hard to believe that your audience cares about what happened in a dinky little town when there's a world war going on. Your program should be about Johnny Groover."

"He'll get plenty of air time on 'The Voice of the People.' But I'd be remiss in my obligation to my listeners if I went back to New York without the story of a young woman who works as a welder in a defense plant, does other things to boost the war effort on the homefront, and also finds time to crack a couple murder cases."

"Please, Mr. Whiteside, I'd rather you didn't do a program about me."

"Very well," he said with a shrug. "Tell me what you know about Johnny Groover."

"I'm sure there's nothing I can say that you haven't heard from Scrappy."

"He didn't go to school with him."

"Johnny was a couple of years behind my graduating class."

"But you did know him?"

"Everyone knew Johnny. He was the quarterback of the football team."

"What's the big deal about that?"

"This will probably sound silly to a sophisticated New Yorker and man about town, but Pennsylvanians are football nuts. Being a star player is a *very* big deal."

"Is that the true reason why the judge who handled the payroll robbery case didn't send Groover to jail?"

"Judge Wooten was obviously touched by the heartfelt plea for leniency from Johnny's father. Besides, Johnny was just a lookout. He didn't brandish the gun."

"Neither did the Perillo boys."

"Sal and Dom each had a record of committing other crimes, either alone, together, or with a couple of other bad apples. The robbery was Johnny Groover's first offense."

The music stopped and Beatrice and Scrappy came to the table.

Breathless and dabbing beads of sweat from his face with a handkerchief, he announced, "Doing the jitterbug is hard work. A man works up a thirst."

"There's plenty of fruit punch," said Beatrice.

Scrappy looked quizzically at Whiteside. "Would you care to join me in a slight tipple at the flowing bowl, Aleck?"

Smiling and patting the side of his suit coat with the flask of brandy tucked in the inside pocket, he replied, "Capital idea!"

As they approached the table with two huge punch bowls, the band offered a scaled-down but still respectable rendition of the Glenn Miller orchestra's theme song, "Moonlight Serenade." With paper cups filled with an orange-colored liquid and spiked with brandy, they watched the faux *Café Americain* quickly fill with people.

"Considering the price of admission," said Aleck as he noted that many were younger than he'd expected, "I feared that this soiree would bring out only the Serutan set. Not that I think of yourself and your lower digestive tract as occasional candidates for the regularity-restorative virtues of the product advertised by one of my sponsors, of course."

"Still having all my teeth and being able to enjoy a breakfast of steak with my scrambled eggs," said Scrappy, "I am also not ready for a daily diet of the cream of wheat that you peddle on your show, either."

With "Moonlight Serenade" finished and the band changing pace by striking up "The Music Goes Round and Round," Aleck declared, "Did you know that I was the inspiration for the number the band is now playing?" Without waiting for a reply, he continued, "One night in the Onyx Club on Fifty-second Street, I asked a trombonist by the name of Mike Riley how he was able to produce such a great sound. He held up his horn, pointed to the mouthpiece, and replied, 'I blow in here and the music goes around and around.' He pointed to the other end of the horn and said, 'And it comes out here.' Later, Mike and trumpeter Ed Farley wrote the song. I demanded that I share in the hit's royalties, of course. But to no avail." He paused for a sip of his drink. Looking around, he continued, "There are enough bright young faces in this crowd that I feel as though I've been thrust back to 1918 and the evening of my senior prom."

Scrappy retorted, "Somehow I find it difficult to believe that Alexander Whiteside was *ever* seventeen. And it's impossible to imagine you tripping the light fantastic to a ragtime tune."

"President Wilson had finally taken off the rose-colored glasses of neutrality and asked for a declaration of war against Germany. Like all the young men at that time, I expected to be called upon to take up arms and that I would be killed in action so that the world would be safe for democracy. We were all passionately patriotic, brimming with romantic notions, and incredibly gullible. In a word, *innocent*."

"After the war did you think of yourself as a member of the lost generation?"

"Good lord no. I may have been disillusioned, but I wasn't a fool. Nor did I feel a need to write *the* great novel about the wastefulness of war. I could have done so, of course."

"Instead, you went to work for a newspaper and became a theater critic."

"In those days when an editor didn't know what to do with someone like me, there was always the drama desk." He grinned impishly. "And the sports pages."

While they were talking, Scrappy was either nodding his head or raising an arm to wave a hand in response to people who'd waved greetings to him.

"I haven't seen so much arm calisthenics," said Aleck as he set his empty cup upon the punch table, "since I rode through the Lower East Side of New York in an open automobile with FDR and Al Smith in the 1936 campaign. If you ever decide to hang up your journalistic spurs to run for mayor of this town, you'll be a shoo-in."

"I think I'll stick to what I do best. I'll be happy to drop dead at my desk in the city room with my reporter's boots on."

"I'm looking forward to reading your account of tonight's festivities."

"I should have given this story to the gal who covers weddings and social occasions. I'm the *Independence*'s politics, sports, and police blotter guy."

Observing Kate approaching them, Aleck said, "Well,

you'll have all those elements in this room, won't you? The mayor of the town will speak in praise of a local war hero who is a former star of the gridiron. But the young man was a participant in the biggest robbery in town history, part of which remains a mystery; what happened to the swag? The situation is positively pregnant with dramatic possibilities."

Kate arrived and grasped Aleck's hand. "Scrappy, you've been hogging Mr. Whiteside long enough," she declared. "Beatrice and I need him to keep us company while we greet the people at the door and wait for the arrival of the guest of honor."

"What am I," said Scrappy, "a potted plant?"

"You may come, too. The doors will open to the public at seven. I've asked Lieutenant Minetta to bring Johnny at half-past."

"When he enters," Beatrice said, "Kate signals the band to strike up 'From the Halls of Montezuma' and we all escort Johnny to the head table."

"Ladies, you are a wonder of organization," said Aleck. "The last time I took part in a receiving line was in 1939 at FDR's home in Hyde Park, New York, for the visit of King George the Sixth and Queen Elizabeth."

"You were there? How exciting," exclaimed Beatrice as they crossed the gymnasium to the closed doors. Seated next to it behind a long table were three women. Members of the Molly Pitcher Society, they were in charge of selling the War Bonds that were the price of admission. "I thought it was brilliant of Mrs. Roosevelt to serve their majesties hot dogs on buns," Beatrice continued. "What a glorious example of determination and courage the king and queen and their daughters provided by remaining in London during those terrible months of the Blitz!"

"I'll never forget being in London during an air raid in 1940," said Aleck as he took the place Kate indicated for him by the closed doors. "I was a house guest of Churchill at Number Ten Downing Street."

Kate looked at him in wide-eyed astonishment. "You're kidding!"

"One never kids about Winston Churchill. When the warning sirens started, we went to Winston's bomb shelter. The bombing lasted all night. Then, a few minutes after the all-clear, he placed a phone call to his tobacconist, Dunhill's in St. James's Square. In that bulldog voice, he demanded a report on the status of his cigars. When he was told that they came through the raid unscathed, he had such a huge grin on his face that you would have thought he had gotten news that the Germans had surrendered. Later in the morning he took me along on one of his famous morale-boosting walking tours of bombed-out London neighborhoods. I told Churchill that the German air raids on the city would backfire on Hitler by hastening the inevitable day when the United States would get into the war. He responded with a truly remarkable prediction. He said, 'That glorious event will come only when the Japanese attack your Pacific fleet at its base in Hawaii. But only after we whip the guttersnipe Hitler and his gang will the Japanese feel the full fury of American wrath.' Those were his exact words as I quoted them on my next broadcast."

"Aleck, you are amazing," exclaimed Beatrice. "I hope that one day I'll read about all of your adventures in your autobiography."

"I've got a title," said Scrappy. "You can call it *Names I Have Dropped*."

Kate looked at her wristwatch. "It's almost seven o'clock." She took a deep breath. "It's time to see if anyone is going to show up."

When Scrappy opened the double doors, he discovered the corridor jammed with people. As they pushed forward, he raised his hands and bellowed, "Take it easy, folks. There's plenty of room, and there are three ladies here to take your money, so there's no need to rush. Just form a line and things will proceed in an orderly way."

As the line formed, the band struck up the Robinsville High School marching band's theme song, "The Band Played On." With the gymnasium slowly filling with people, it offered a medley of the school's football "fight" songs. Drawing a cigar from his pocket to the raucous strains of "Buckle Down Winsocki," Scrappy muttered, "What is this, a pep rally?"

When most of the tables were claimed, the band switched to dance music, beginning with the Artie Shaw hit "Moonglow."

Hearing the music as he waited in the back of the Buick parked across Second Avenue, Johnny Groover observed a line of people waiting patiently to get into the school. Seated beside Lieutenant Minetta, he nervously drummed his fingers on his knees and demanded, "What the fuck are we sitting here for?"

"The women who planned this, Kate Fallon and the lady who owns the bookstore, told me they want you to make a grand entrance at seven-thirty sharp."

Johnny nodded toward the school and laughed. "Look

at all those people. Most of them I don't even *know*. This is nuts!"

"Stop getting yourself all worked up. You'll have a swell time."

Turning abruptly, he pleaded, "What do you say we get the hell out of here? I know a nice quiet bar. Let's get falling-down drunk."

"That's a prescription for a couple of courts-martial if I ever heard one. They'll nail you for going AWOL and me for dereliction of duty. But this time nobody will be influenced by a plea for mercy from your father. If they don't order us keelhauled, we'll spend the duration of the war in adjoining cells in the brig, me at the Naval base in Philly and you in the Marine base at Parris Island, South Carolina. Thanks, but no thanks."

Johnny looked again at the line. "Most of the people over there believe jail is where I should have gone two years ago."

"If that's so, why are they forking out their hard-earned money to salute you?"

"For the same reason they buy tickets to gawk at the freaks in carnival sideshows."

Having listened with welling anger in the front seat, the driver suddenly turned to look into the rear of the car. With glaring eyes, he said, "You listen to me, kid. The reason all these people have come out is because the government says you're a war hero. Maybe you are and maybe you ain't. But my guess is that most of those people you say you don't know have boys in the service. I've got a son in the Army myself. And right now in their eyes, and in mine, you are as close as they can get to telling those kids how much they miss 'em. So if shaking hands with you will make just one of those people feel better, then you damn well better get your ass across this street and do your duty. Because if you don't, even if you are a tough guy who mowed down a couple of hundred Japs, I'm gonna yank you out of this car, sock you in your ungrateful kisser, and drag you over there by the scruff of your neck."

"All right, all right," Johnny exclaimed. "I'm going."

Laughing as he opened the door on his side of the Buick, Minetta said to the driver, "Mister, I couldn't have said it better myself. Come inside and I'll buy you a drink."

The driver shrugged. "Thanks, but I make it a policy not to drink when I drive. But after, if the kid still feels like tying one on, I'd be happy to drive you to a bar that my uncle owns out by the Army hospital, where I'm sure the drinks will be on the house."

"We just might take you up on that."

"And about the trouble the kid got into a couple of years ago? I doubt that there's a soul in this town who doesn't think that he more than made up for it by what he did on Guadalcanal."

"When this shindig is over," said Minetta as he left the car, "you should tell him that."

An Evening
in Casablanca

THREE RAPID, LOUD raps on the door to Scrappy Mac-
Farland's room interrupted Scrappy's narrative and a
dowdy-looking woman in a gray smock barged in. Carrying a tray, she declared, "Time for your lunch, honey."

With a disgruntled expression, Scrappy growled,
"Can't you see I've got a visitor?"

Steely in eye and voice, she snapped, "If you don't eat
it now—"

Scrappy wagged a hand impatiently. "Just park the tray
and go."

"Very well," she said, leaving it on a bedside table, "but
I don't want to hear any griping from you about it being
cold."

As she departed, I couldn't help laughing.

He glared at me. "What's so damn amusing?"

"I'm sorry. That scene could have come right out of
House Guest from Hell."

"What are you talking about?"

"Your battle with the attendant reminded me of the play and movie that were supposedly based on your friend Aleck. There's a running battle between the main character and a nurse."

"Oh that. The difference between that character and me is that he ultimately got to leave his confinement by walking out of the house on his own two legs. The only way I'm leaving here is in a pine box. Now where was I?"

"Aleck was saying that the evening at the junior high school gymnasium was pregnant with dramatic possibilities."

"He always saw things through the eyes of a theater critic."

"I think that on that evening Aleck was right on the mark."

Scrappy smiled. "Are you a reader, young man? Of novels, I mean."

"I'm sure I could do better on that score."

"Aleck devoured them. When he made that remark about pregnant possibilities, he was no doubt remembering similar scenes in fiction that he'd read. For instance, the parties in *The Great Gatsby,* by his friend F. Scott Fitzgerald."

"Aleck knew him?"

"Aleck knew everybody who was anybody. And more than a few of his friends got to *be* somebody *because* of Aleck. He was a shameless booster of people he liked, or people whose work that he approved of. A rave notice in an Aleck Whiteside column could turn an unknown into a star. He did the trick for John O'Hara when O'Hara finally took Aleck's advice and tried his hand at a novel. Before that, O'Hara was a short-story writer. Aleck goaded him so much that he locked himself in a hotel room and wrote *Appointment in Samara*. Aleck's review heaped it with laurels and it became a best-seller. Talking of pregnant possibilities at a party! In the book one of the guests throws a drink in another guest's face. The novel is still in print. I suggest you read it. You may find it relevant to your purpose in grilling me about Johnny Groover."

"Do I take it that something dramatic *did* happen that night?"

Scrappy turned slightly in his chair and peered across the room at the lunch tray. "I might as well take a look at what the Wicked Witch of the West brought."

"Stay put," I said. "I'll get it for you."

"Whatever it is, you can help me get rid of it."

"Thanks, but I'm not hungry."

"I have discovered that the older I get, the less I eat," he said as I fetched the meal of meat loaf, green beans, mashed potatoes, and a glass of milk. "That's pretty amazing, considering that when I was your age I used to have a sixteen-ounce steak with two baked potatoes drowned in butter, plus apple pie à la mode for dessert every night for dinner at the Vale-Rio Diner. When the government imposed meat rationing during the war, one of the things I missed most was that nightly steak dinner. Then I learned that if you had connections in the black market, getting meat was no problem. Or tires for your car. Sugar. Butter. You name it, some black marketeer had as much as you wanted. I never understood how some people could cash in on the war while our young men were being killed."

"The black market wouldn't have existed if people didn't support it," I said, handing him the tray. "It's like the problem with narcotics today. If there was no demand for drugs, there'd be no suppliers."

Scrappy sniffed the meat loaf, made a face, and handed me the tray. "I think this meat is left over from the Second World War."

"If you're not going to eat," I said, taking the glass of milk from the tray, "you should at least drink this."

"Cow juice! I hate the stuff. Away with it," he said while I carried the tray to the bedside table. "The only dairy product Harry Groover delivered to my door was a pound of butter, twice a week. That was before the war, of course. What I got during it was oleomargarine. Horrible! It wasn't like the product you see in stores today. Back then if you bought it artificially colored, there was a federal tax of a dime a pound. But if you bought it uncolored, the tax was a quarter of a cent. It came with a little packet of coloring that you mixed in with your hands. I tried mixing it once and, after that, ate the stuff plain. Kate Fallon told me a funny story about margarine and her dad. She said when he came home from work one day, he decided to make a lettuce and tomato sandwich—there wasn't any meat to put in it, you see—so he lathered two pieces of bread with what he thought was a block of uncolored margarine setting on the kitchen counter. Only after he'd eaten the sandwich did he find out it was a pound of lard! When Kate told me that story, she was in tears from laughing so hard."

"She must have been quite a remarkable young woman."

"Indeed she was," said Scrappy with a faraway look in his eyes. "And never more so than in her cardboard and crepe paper version of an evening in Casablanca."

As he settled back and made himself more comfortable in his armchair, something in the expression on his face and his tone of voice cautioned me not to interrupt him . . .

When the band suddenly stopped in the middle of a pretty darned good rendition of "I Don't Want to Set the World on Fire" and struck up the Marine Corps march, all eyes in the gymnasium turned toward the door. What they saw was Johnny Groover looking as if he was a deer in the middle of a road that was caught in the headlights of a speeding car. As I watched him, I wondered how anybody who could look so scared had ever managed to do what he'd done on Guadalcanal. Then Kate Fallon stepped forward and said something to him that made him smile a little and appear to relax a bit.

By then the people were applauding and cheering so loud that they all but drowned out the music. They kept it up as Kate led Johnny and Lieutenant Minetta, followed by Bea Bradshaw, Aleck Whiteside, and me, to the head table. Mayor Cantrell was there with his wife and a couple of members of the town council. Always the politician, and being up for reelection that year, the mayor had a photographer on hand to snap his picture shaking hands with Johnny while he babbled about how Johnny had made the town feel proud.

That was true for most of the people, but not for all of them. At the newspaper we'd gotten a few letters-to-the-editor from folks who expressed outrage and disgust that a kid who'd been involved in an armed robbery was having the red carpet rolled out for him. A couple of the letters had gone so far as to claim that the story of Johnny

Groover having single-handedly killed two hundred Japs had been cooked up in Washington on orders from FDR, just as Roosevelt, according to them, had known the Japs were planning the attack on Pearl Harbor and did nothing to stop it because he wanted to get the country into the war to save England's skin. Can you believe that some people still believe in such a bullshit theory?

Anyway, when the crowd in the gym finally stopped clapping, the band went back to playing dance music and our guest of honor seemed a lot more at ease. I still felt sorry for him, though, because people started coming to the table and talking to him. I could tell by the look on his face that he didn't know most of them. But that didn't keep him from being polite, smiling, shaking their hands, and even signing autographs for a few of them.

Some of the ones who came to the table were friends of his, of course. Many of them were apparently former girl-friends. I remember one of them vividly because of the fire-engine-red dress she had on, and for what they said. He was sitting between me and Coach Franklin, so I couldn't help but hear them. He mentioned a letter he'd gotten from her and she started going on about how sorry she was that she'd hurt him, but he just laughed and told her that it didn't matter because he'd known her well enough to have expected her to waste no time in finding somebody else. With that, her face turned as red as her dress and she practically ran from the room.

With so many old friends and strangers crowding around the table, the situation got so bad that Kate attempted to rescue him from all the attention by asking him to dance. But when they got onto the dance floor, other couples stopped and stood off to the side, so that Kate and

Johnny were out there all alone as if they were Fred Astaire and Ginger Rogers.

When they came back to the table, Kate and Beatrice put their heads together and decided that the only way to take the pressure off Johnny was to get the formalities over with, so Kate went up on the bandstand and asked everyone to sit down. She explained that there would be some brief remarks from Mayor Cantrell, Alexander Whiteside, and the man of the hour.

"After these brief speeches," she said, "I'm sure you will all want to allow Johnny to enjoy the evening without further interruptions."

With that, the program went as planned. Mayor Cantrell gave his speech, as did Aleck and Johnny, all of which were warmly received. Then everyone pretty much did as Kate requested by leaving Johnny in peace. He spent a lot of the time gabbing with Coach Franklin about the football team. I recall him telling Franklin about feeling disappointed that Richie Zale wasn't there. The coach explained that Richie's shift at the steel mill was the four-to-midnight, but that he was sure that before Johnny had to leave town, the three of them would all be able to get together like they used to in the old days.

My impression was that Johnny had gotten over his nervousness and was having a pretty good time. Kate and Beatrice saw to it that he had some of the food. I had a feeling that at first he didn't know quite what to make of Aleck. That changed when Johnny said in an aside to Aleck that the fruit punch was a poor excuse for a drink and Aleck immediately resolved the problem by slipping Johnny the flask.

Around eleven o'clock with the crowd thinning out, our

esteemed police chief put a damper on the festivities. Until then, he and his right arm, Officer Todd Doebling, had been lurking around the edges of the crowd. But suddenly, there he was at the head table with a Dick Tracy look on his face and saying to Johnny, "I need to have a talk with you."

"Is that so?" Johnny said. "What about?"

"You know damned well what about."

With that, Kate Fallon jumped to her feet with a "you're getting my Irish up" look on her face. Jutting out her jaw, she said, "Sir, this is hardly the time or place."

Beatrice Bradshaw exclaimed, "Indeed it is not, Tom."

Unfurling the flag of the U.S. Navy, metaphorically speaking, Lieutenant Minetta said, "And whatever conversation you wish to have with Sergeant Groover will not take place without me present."

"Lieutenant, my business with this man has nothing to do with you, the Navy, or the Marine Corps, so just butt out."

Coach Franklin joined in with, "Gentlemen, please. Let's not have a scene."

Of course, that's just what had been created. The remaining guests looked on in a state of shock. Aware of this, Chief Detwiler gave a shrug of his broad shoulders and said through a tight smile, "Very well, *Sergeant* Groover, our little talk can wait. But I expect to see you in my office at police headquarters tomorrow morning at ten o'clock. If you're not there, Officer Doebling will be ordered to find you and bring you in."

Minetta demanded, "By what authority?"

"Mine."

"You have no legal authority over a member of the United States Marine Corps."

With that Johnny exclaimed, "Just shut the hell up, all of you."

"Listen to me, Johnny," said Minetta. "You don't have to talk to this guy."

Coach Franklin butted in at that point to say the same thing, that Johnny did not have to talk to the police, and that he, Franklin, wished he wouldn't.

"It's all right," Johnny said. "I want to talk to him."

Detwiler smiled triumphantly. "Good. My office. Tomorrow morning at ten."

Scrappy took a deep breath and gave me an inscrutable smile. "That little drama was not the ending that Kate Fallon envisioned for her evening in Casablanca," he said. "It was an ironic moment. That dialogue between Johnny and Chief Detwiler that night was right out of a scene in the movie, the one in which the Nazi officer ordered Victor Laslo to report to the prefect's office in the morning to discuss the letters of transit."

"As I recall, he and Ilsa Lund kept the appointment," I said. "Did Johnny?"

"There you go again, wanting to skip ahead to the last page!"

—— Part 4 ——

The Bodyguard

Show me a hero and I'll write you a tragedy.

—F. Scott Fitzgerald

24

As Chief Detwiler and Officer Doebling walked away, the band began the traditional song to signal the evening was over. With only eight couples taking the floor to dance to "Good Night, Sweetheart," Kate stared angrily at Chief Detwiler's broad back.

"What colossal nerve that man has," she exclaimed as he and Doebling left the gym. "He hasn't a shred of consideration. He picked that moment just to spoil everybody's fun."

"That's not true," said Scrappy. "Tom can be pretty uncouth, but if he had wanted to ruin the evening's fun, he wouldn't have waited till the party was winding down. He could have made his move when everyone's eyes were on Johnny when he arrived."

"Well, if you ask me," said Coach Franklin angrily, "it would have been just as damned rude of him to do it then."

Kate nodded her head. "What he did was just outrageous! I intend to complain about his brutish behavior to Mayor Cantrell. And then I'm going to tell the chief what I think of him."

"You can always tell a cop," said Aleck. "But not much."

"Let it go, Kate," Johnny implored. "You're making too big a deal out of this."

Lieutenant Minetta said, "You don't have to talk to him. The police have no legal right to claim jurisdiction over you. If he wants to talk to you in his official capacity, he is required to make the request to the Marine Corps. And you have the right to have a Marine Corps lawyer with you during any questioning."

"Look, I don't mind going to police headquarters tomorrow. If he hadn't said he wanted to talk with me, I would have asked to see him. So I won't need a lawyer to hold my hand."

"My advice," said Coach Franklin, "is that you do nothing until the lieutenant has spoken to someone higher up about this matter."

Johnny clapped him in the shoulder. "I've already done that. But don't worry, I know what I'm doing and everything is going to be fine." Turning to Kate, he said, "If this has spoiled anyone's fun, I'm sorry. Thanks to you and Mrs. Bradshaw and everybody who arranged for the party. I've had a hell of a good time tonight. Now it's over and it's long past this Marine's usual time for lights out, so I wish you all good night."

A few moments later as Johnny stood at the top of the school's front steps to light up a Camel cigarette, Minetta said, "What did you mean in there when you said that you'd spoken to someone higher up?"

"Don't worry, Lieutenant, I wasn't referring to anyone in the Navy's chain of command. I'll tell you about it, but not now." He blew a plume of smoke and watched it swirl away on a gust of cold night air. "Did you have any of that punch they were serving in there? I think horse piss would have tasted better. Thank God for Aleck Whiteside's handy hip flask! Whaddaya say we go somewhere and get something to drink with a kick in it?"

"Matter of fact," said Minetta as he put on gloves, "we've got an invitation for drinks on the house. Our driver told me his uncle owns a bar near the Army hospital, wherever that is."

"I know the place," said Johnny, bounding down the steps. "It's called the Roadhouse. It's kind of a dive. Honest drinks and disreputable women, too." He barked a laugh. "And both are just what I'm feeling horny for."

"If it's none of my damn business, tell me," said Minetta as they walked to the car, "but who was the girl in the red dress that you were whispering to?"

"It is none of your business, but I don't mind telling you. Her name is Pat Roberts. She and I had something hot and heavy going in high school, and for a little while after that. We even talked about getting hitched. But when I went off to fight for democracy and the American way of life, for her it was a case of out of sight, out of mind. Her Dear John letter caught up to me a few days before I shoved off for the Canal."

"And she had the gall to show her face tonight?"

"She wanted to know if I'd gotten the letter."

"That is one hell of a self-centered bitch."

Johnny flipped away the Camel and watched it sail in an arc to a landing on a patch of snow at the edge of the lawn. "Pat is certainly that," he said with a little laugh. "But she was a really great lay. Anyway, by the time I got the Dear John, I'd realized that marrying her would have been the biggest mistake of my life."

"Except getting involved in that stupid holdup."

"It *was* stupid," Johnny said as he got into the back of the car, "but think of it this way. If I hadn't gone along with the Perillo boys and Pete Slattery, I wouldn't be in the Marines and you wouldn't be standing here and looking forward to getting your ashes hauled by a pickup at the Roadhouse, as I'm sure you are!"

The driver asked, "Did I hear you say we're going to the Roadhouse?"

"Indeed you did, my man," Johnny replied with a grin. "So make it full speed ahead and damn the torpedoes."

25

OPPOSITE THE WESTERN perimeter of the George Washington Army Hospital at the intersection of Route 29 and Coldstream Road, the low concrete building had a red and yellow neon sign that proclaimed ROADHOUSE BAR AND GRILL. A parking lot in front and one on the left side were filled with automobiles.

"Before the war this place was a country store," explained the driver as he pulled into a space near the door. "It was run by an elderly couple whose farm was lost during the Depression when the Farmer's Bank foreclosed on their mortgage. When word got around that the Army was going to build the hospital, my uncle made them an offer to take it over that was enough to let them move to Florida and retire near their daughter. Of course, Uncle Jake didn't tell them his plans for the place. They were Mennonites, you see, and if they'd known that it was going to be a tavern, they wouldn't have sold it to him. Now it's a goldmine."

"Will you be joining us?" asked Johnny.

"Thanks, but like I told the lieutenant, I make it a policy not to drink when I have to drive people around. But I will go in and tell Uncle Jake that I told you the drinks were on the house. He'll be thrilled to know that you're in his place, Sergeant. It's not every day that he gets a war hero in the joint."

"I'd appreciate it if you wouldn't make a big deal of that," said Johnny. "I'm getting a little tired of all the fuss."

"I'll tell Uncle Jake to be sure that nobody bothers you."

"That courtesy needn't extend to keeping *everyone* away from us," said Minetta with a laugh and an elbow jabbed into Johnny's side. "There's no objection to good-looking women."

"Gotcha, fellas! But if it don't work out to your satisfaction inside, I can take you to a very nice house near the freight depot on the south end of town."

"Would that be Annie's place?" asked Johnny.

"That's right. But Annie doesn't run it anymore."

"Don't tell me she got religion!"

"She got a proposition she couldn't refuse and sold out about a year ago. The operation is in the hands of some wiseguys from Philadelphia, but it's still known as Annie's house. I think she made a big mistake in selling out. What with the hospital bringing in so many soldiers who are stationed there, and some of the patients who come into town on Saturday night passes, business is as hot as a house on fire."

"We'll keep Annie's in mind," said Minetta as they got out of the car, "but I doubt that our horny hero will end up having to pay for it."

The driver cackled a laugh. "I see what you mean. Since he's so famous, a woman might be so impressed that she'd pay him."

Going in, they found a dimly lighted room crowded with young men in Army uniforms. All in enlisted ranks, they crowded the long bar at the back of the room. Several older men in civilian attire at the bar looked as if they were also Army. A low ceiling was almost obscured by a cloud of blue tobacco smoke. Two rows of small round tables with red-and-white-checkered cloths and tiny, shaded lamps flanked a small, tiled dance floor with no one dancing. Most of the tables were occupied by groups of soldiers, but at a few of the tables the men enjoyed the company of women. There were none at the bar because the laws of the Commonwealth of Pennsylvania did not permit it. A Wurlitzer jukebox blared "Wabash Cannonball" by Roy Acuff.

Raising his voice to be heard over it as they pushed through the crowd, Johnny said, "I hope you don't object to hillbilly music, Lieutenant. It's all they have on the jukebox."

"Ah, you've been in this joint before."

"One time only. A friend brought me here the night before I left for the Marines."

"You're only twenty-one now. How did you get them to let you in?"

"The friend vouched for me."

"I guess I can put up with hillbilly songs for a while."

"After a couple of Roadhouse drinks, you probably won't give a damn what's playing."

"You can have all the drinks your heart desires," said Minetta as they reached the bar, "but as long as I'm responsible for you, one has to be my limit."

"Oh come on, who's gonna know? You have my word as a Marine that I'll never tell. Let yourself go, for cripes sake. What happens if I get lucky with one of these ladies? I hope you're not expecting me to bring you along. I wouldn't mind a threesome, but—no offense—you're not exactly my type. I adhere strictly to the rule against officers socializing with enlisted men."

"We'll cross the bridge of you getting lucky if we get to it."

"Not if, Lieutenant." Raising a hand in the hope of catching the attention of a bartender, he said, "*When* we get to it. What's the point in my being a war hero with the medals to prove it if I can't get laid?"

The bartender arrived. "What'll it be? The boss says I'm to serve you all the drinks you want on the house."

"I'll have a beer," said Minetta.

"Draft or bottle?"

"Bottle, please."

"Make mine a Seven and Seven," said Johnny. "Double."

Minetta cracked a smile. "You *are* in a hurry."

As the record in the Wurlitzer changed to Gene Autry's "Deep in the Heart of Texas," Johnny turned slightly to survey the women at the tables. "I had a buddy from San Antonio who was nuts about this song," he said, noticing a blonde in a yellow Lana Turner sweater who was talking to a corporal but looking past him and giving himself the once-over. "His name was Billy Lee Austin. He said he was related to the man they named the city after."

The bartender set up their drinks.

"Billy Lee was so damn proud of being a Texan," said Johnny with a little laugh as he picked up the Seven and Seven, "that he had a map of the state tattooed on his chest. Then poor Billy Lee went and got his head blown off by a mortar round in the fight for Henderson Field." He took a gulp of the drink. "Billy Lee used to drink tequila. Billy Lee getting killed like that really pissed me off!"

"Were you thinking about Billy Lee when you grabbed that machine gun?"

Johnny grunted. "The only things in my head at that moment were all those fuckin' Japs rushing toward me and a hope that the damned ammo belt wouldn't run out of rounds. What do you think of the dame in the yellow sweater?"

"She certainly seems to be interested in you."

"Working girl?"

"More than likely."

"Have you ever gone with one?"

"I'm married."

"Really? I didn't know."

"No reason for you to."

"You've never strayed from the reservation?"

"Nope."

"Ever think about it?"

"A couple of times," said Minetta as the woman in the sweater abandoned the corporal. "But I knew if I went beyond thinking that my wife would somehow know about it. Women can sense it. I also knew that if I were unfaithful, I'd hate myself."

"If you were to go astray," Johnny said as the woman made her way between dancers, "and your wife sensed it and confronted you, would you own up to it?"

"I don't know. I hope I'm never put in that position."

"Wouldn't you have to confess it to your priest?"

"I guess so."

"It must be tough being a Catholic."

Before Minetta could reply, the woman was at Johnny's side. Looking him up and down, she asked, "Don't I know you from somewhere?"

Johnny smiled. "I don't think so."

"You look real familiar."

"If we'd met, I'm sure I'd remember."

"Well, we have now. I'm Honey."

Johnny leaned close to her and whispered, "I'll bet you are."

Minetta groaned and turned away.

She edged between them. "So what's your name?"

"Johnny."

"I don't get to see many Marines in this place."

"I'm home on leave."

"So you're a local boy!"

"Born and raised."

"I'm not from around here. I wonder why you look so familiar."

"Does it matter?"

She studied his face a moment, then took a step back. "In the newspaper! I seen you in the paper. You're that hero who got written up so much. Wow, what an honor!"

"Hey, it's no big deal. When I'm not being a hero, I'm

just another guy. I've got a head, two arms, two legs, two feet, and all the other equipment you'd expect. But no angel's wings, I assure you."

Minetta let out a laugh.

The music changed to "I'm Thinking Tonight of My Blue Eyes."

Johnny took a sip of his drink and said, "Somebody in here is sure a Gene Autry fan."

"I love this song," said Honey as she moved closer to him. "You've got blue eyes. Wanna dance . . . Blue Eyes?"

"I warn you, I'm a little rusty."

"Dancing's like riding a bicycle," she said, taking his hand and tugging him toward the dance floor. "You never forget how to do it. The same's true for making love."

As they moved away from the bar, Minetta grinned and muttered, "Way to go, Sergeant!"

The bartender bent close to whisper, "I'm not one to stick his nose in, Lieutenant, but that dame is bad news. She's the type who'll roll a guy. Like I said, it's none of my business, but if that kid was a friend of mine, I'd see that he didn't leave with her. If he's looking to get laid, I'll be happy to point him to better pickin's."

"Thanks, my friend. I'll keep that in mind."

"He seems like a nice guy. I'd hate to see something bad happen now that it seems like he's straightened himself out. I assume you know about the mess he got himself into a couple of years ago?"

Minetta took a swig of beer. "I do."

"I always thought the only reason he got into trouble was because he fell in with a bad crowd. That guy Slattery was always bad news. The proof of that is the way the bastard took it on the lam and left everybody who pulled that stupid heist to take the rap. Good riddance to bad rubbish, I say. I guess being in the Marines, the kid finally grew up."

Minetta turned to watch Johnny and Honey dance. "Getting shot three times also helped."

"If you want me to, I can give that broad the heave-ho."

"Let's just wait and see what develops."

"I can arrange for another girl to cut in. Don't get me wrong, I'm not a pimp. I just don't want a kid who nearly got killed fighting for our country to get hurt if I can prevent it."

When the song ended, Johnny and the woman went to a table.

Setting aside his bottle of beer, Minetta said to the bartender, "I guess I'd better go over there and pull my rank." But as he stepped away from the bar, Johnny suddenly got up from the table and left the woman sitting there. "From the look on his face," he said to the bartender as Johnny strode toward them, "I'd say that neither of us will have to intervene."

"I can't believe it," exclaimed Johnny when he reached the bar. "She told me her price was a hundred bucks, and that's not even for the whole night! What in hell does she think that a Marine gets paid in a month? I'm horny, but I'm not *that* fuckin' desperate."

Minetta patted his shoulder sympathetically. "I think she was too old for you anyway."

Glaring at her, Johnny replied, "Yeah, she's got to be at least thirty." With a chuckle, he added, "She's got great bazooms, though, don't you think?"

Minetta shrugged. "If they're real."

Johnny's glare became a squint. "Falsies? Nah. I gave one of 'em a squeeze."

"They're doing great things these days with synthetic rubber."

The bartender asked, "You ready for another double Seven and Seven, Sarge?"

Still peering across the room and watching an Army top sergeant approaching Honey's table, he gave an emphatic nod. "You said it, pal," he said, turning away, "but hold the freakin' Seven-Up. No, wait. Make it tequila. Billy Lee Austin used to say that if you want to get real drunk, you gotta drink tequila. He used to say it puts hair on your chest, which was very funny, because the only thing I ever saw on Billy Lee's was a damn tattooed map of Texas. What time is it, by the way?"

Minetta looked at his wristwatch. "It's a quarter to midnight."

"That gives me four more hours to get totally sloshed, and ten before H-Hour when I have my rendezvous with destiny at police headquarters."

26

STANDING IN THE doorway of the chief of police's office, Officer Todd Doebling found Detwiler seated at his desk and hunched over a thick bundle of papers. "If there's nothing more that you need me for, boss," he said, "I'll be taking off."

Detwiler looked up. "No, you go ahead on home. But be back here at nine o'clock."

Doebling stepped into the office. "Is that the file on the payroll robbery?"

"I thought that before I have my little chat with Groover in the morning, I'd better go over the transcript from the last time the lying son of a bitch was in here. As sure as God made little green apples, he knows where that money is, and I intend to pry it out of him. If that idiot judge hadn't let Groover off the hook, I could have recovered the money. I pleaded with Judge Wooten to continue the case and hold off sentencing for a week or so. I was certain that all I needed was a little more time to squeeze it out of that kid."

"Excuse me for saying so," said Doebling, "but I can't see what good it'll do to try to talk to Groover now. I appreciate that you're upset on account of that case being the only case you haven't completely closed, but the way I see it, Groover is going to show up tomorrow with that Navy officer who's baby-sitting him. My guess is, he'll order Groover to keep his trap shut. And how's it going to look if Minetta decides to yell his head off to Scrappy MacFarland about the police hounding a war hero?"

"I'm willing to take my chances on that. You just be here at nine o'clock."

Ten minutes before shift-change time in the rolling mill of the steel plant the foreman of the four-to-midnight shift, Mike O'Donnell, was surprised that Richie Zale had turned down an opportunity to pick up time-and-a-half pay for staying on the job two more hours to help finish a run of I beams for the Philadelphia Navy Yard.

"You know I'm always looking for overtime," he'd explained, "but both the kids have been sick and Millie's worn out from not getting enough rest. I've promised her I'd get home at the regular time so I can be up in the morning to handle the kids and Millie can stay in bed to catch some extra sleep."

"I understand completely," said O'Donnell. "And seeing that you didn't ask for the night off so you could go to the big party for your pal Johnny, I won't order you to stay, even though we are shorthanded."

Consequently, when the whistle on the roof of the mill signaled midnight, Richie went to his Dodge in the employees' parking lot and drove away. Stopping at a phone booth five minutes later, he called his house and told Millie, "Honey, I won't be home for a few more hours. Mike's' asked me to work till two o'clock. How are the kids?"

Sounding irritated, she replied, "They're quiet now, but they were a handful all night. I had a devil of a time getting them into bed."

"Well, you go to bed, too. So I won't disturb you when I come in, I'll lay down on the parlor couch till you get up in the morning."

Fifteen minutes after Richie hung up the phone, he rang Coach Franklin's doorbell. When the door opened, he found Franklin wearing a long green bathrobe. Stepping inside, he said, "I can only stay till four." Going into the parlor, he asked, "Johnny's not here?"

"When I spoke to him at the party and asked him to join us here after you got off work, he seemed excited by the idea. But evidently he's changed his mind. It appears that it's going to be just us two chickens."

"Maybe he's just running a little late."

"The party at the gym ended over an hour ago," Franklin said. He sat dejectedly on the couch. "If he was coming, he'd have been here by now."

"Knowing Johnny," Richie replied, sitting next to him, "he's probably getting himself laid somewhere."

Franklin giggled. "I trust he's mastered the use of rubbers by now."

Richie looked at his watch. "I'm sure he'll show up sooner or later."

"In the meantime," said Franklin, "may I get you something to drink?"

"A jolt of Jack Daniels if you've got some."

"I picked up a fifth at the State Store this afternoon," said Franklin as he got up to go into the kitchen, "and a bottle of Seagram's Seven for Johnny. If he ever comes."

"Don't worry, he'll be here. How was the party?"

"The gymnasium was jammed. The entire place was done up like an exotic nightclub. I found it romantic in a tacky kind of way. Johnny, of course, *ruled* it like a conquering hero. The only sour note came from our chief of police. He demanded that Johnny go down to headquarters in the morning to be interviewed yet again about the late unpleasantness."

Richie followed Franklin into the kitchen. "Maybe that explains why Johnny's not here. He could have skipped town."

Pouring the Jack Daniels into a tall glass halfway, Franklin frowned as he said, "Leave without seeing you again? I hardly think so, dear boy."

Richie took the drink. "Perhaps he hasn't been able to shake off his bodyguard."

"Yes," said Franklin, pouring himself a whiskey, "that's probably it." He held up his glass. "A toast to the glorious days of yesteryear."

Midnight in Beatrice Bradshaw's cosy bedroom had been marked by a dulcet-toned voice from the radio announcing, "It's twelve o'clock Bulova watch time. B-U-

L-O-V-A. Bulova! The official time keeper of our armed forces fighting for freedom around the world. America runs on Bulova time." This was followed by another mellow voice introducing " 'Music Until Dawn,' with your host for the wee hours, Michael Ludlum."

As the program began with the Freddy Martin Orchestra recording of Tchaikovsky's *Piano Concerto in B Flat,* popularized with the title "Tonight We Love," Beatrice settled deeply into the pillows of her bed to read a collection of Alexander Whiteside magazine essays that had first appeared in *Vanity Fair, Collier's, The Saturday Evening Post,* and *The New Yorker.* With a foreword, "Recreations for the Noble Mind," by Rex Stout, author of the Nero Wolfe novels and a Whiteside friend, the amusingly eye-catching title of the book was "The Fine Art of Murder." Its table of contents promised "The Smutty Nose Horrors," "The Murder of Helen Jewett," "The Kidnaping of Baby Lindbergh," "I Was a J. Edgar Hoover G-Man for a Day," "Where I'd Look for Judge Crater," and "But Did Lizzie Borden Really Do It?"

Yet none of these fetching invitations to explore the brilliant mind of Aleck Whiteside could keep Beatrice's thoughts from dwelling on the shockingly bad manners of Police Chief Tom Detwiler in disturbing a delightful evening by pestering poor Johnny Groover about a crime that hardly anyone still cared a whit about. All those who committed it had been punished, save one, either by being sent to prison and reform school or, in Johnny Groover's case, presented with a Hobson's choice between incarceration and the possibility of being killed in action. The money that was stolen remained missing, but

everyone who had followed the case knew that it had disappeared along with Peter Slattery. The true mastermind
of the crime, he had cleverly tipped off the police to the
involvement of the three Perillo boys and Johnny
Groover as he was making his escape. Everyone familiar
with the affair believed this to be true and that Johnny
had played a minor role in the episode, for which he had
more than paid a penalty by suffering three wounds in
battle.

Determined to put the matter out of her mind, she
opened Aleck's book to Rex Stout's foreword and read, "It
has been said that the detective story is the recreation of
noble minds. I do not recall who it was who said it, but it
could very well have been the author of the essays in the
book you now hold in your hand. We know that Alexander Whiteside is an expert on the art of murder, at least
those committed by others in reality and fiction, for he has
told us this is so himself. He has also insisted that when it
comes to noble minds, his ranks right up there. So who am
I to quibble?"

With a little laugh, Beatrice read on to the accompani-
ment of Tchaikovsky as interpreted by the Freddy Martin
Orchestra. By the time she'd finished Stout's brief dis-
course, "Music Until Dawn" was presenting the orchestra
of Raymond Scott playing the appropriately titled "In the
Hush of the Night."

Seething with anger at Chief Detwiler's boorish behavior, Kate Fallon had entered her bedroom and looked at
the unfinished letter to Mike on her dressing table. Her
impulse was to continue it with an account of how terribly

embarrassed she'd been for Johnny, but she suddenly felt exhausted and threw herself onto her bed. Barely a minute later, she fell asleep.

Lying prone on her bed, still in the red dress, Patricia Roberts was going over everything that had gone wrong. At lunch with Bobby Gordon at the General Washington Hotel, instead of getting an engagement ring she'd been accused of still being in love with Johnny Groover. Then at the party at the junior high school gym she'd found out that Johnny had received her letter, but rather than being heartbroken, he'd had a good laugh about it with a Marine Corps buddy named Billy Lee something or other.

"Damn you, Bobby Gordon, and double-damn you, Johnny Groover," she cried at the very moment her nosy sister breezed into the bedroom.

Stopping short, Nancy asked, "What's the matter with you?"

"Men are what's the matter," Pat replied. "Now get out of here and leave me alone."

Backing out the door, Nancy huffed, "Well, excuse me for caring. I'll just go to my room and lie down and die."

Rolling onto her back, Pat said, "I wish that's what Johnny had done on Guadalcanal."

Standing behind Scrappy MacFarland at his desk in the city room of the Robinsville *Independence,* Alexander Whiteside peered over Scrappy's shoulder as stubby fingers typed:

Last night in the gymnasium of Memorial Junior High School, which was handsomely decorated to simulate the nightclub in the recent Humphrey Bogart movie *Casablanca,* the proud people of our town saluted the

"That's crap," said Scrappy. He yanked the sheet of yellow paper from the typewriter, crumpled it into a ball, and flung it to the floor.

"It certainly was," said Aleck as Scrappy rolled another sheet into the Underwood. "You can do much better than that."

Scrappy tilted back in his swivel chair, plucked a cigar from his shirt pocket, and stared at the paper. A moment later the unlit cigar was in the right side of his mouth and the fingers were battering the keyboard as Aleck read:

If Hitler, Tojo and Mussolini had been in the Memorial Junior High gym last night to witness the people of Robinsville saluting Sergeant Johnny Groover, they would have seen why their crackpot dreams of world conquest are doomed. The people of our town who turned out to greet the handsome, boyishly shy hero of Guadalcanal demonstrated that it's not the industrial might of the Allies that's going to defeat the Axis, but millions of young men like Johnny Groover who are prepared to lay down their lives to stop them.

"Very much better," said Aleck, going around to the front of Scrappy's desk to settle his bulky body into a straight-back chair that, like most of the furniture in the city room, appeared to date to the First World War. Looking round, he sighed and said, "You're a lucky man, Scrappy. I envy what you have."

"What I've got," said Scrappy as he typed furiously, "is a deadline."

"Yes, of course. I'm sorry for disturbing you. I'll be quiet."

The typing stopped. "There's a room full of typewriters and plenty of copy paper. Make yourself useful. Grab a desk and bat out a sidebar giving the readers of the *Independence* the inimitable Alexander Whiteside slant on the night's festivities. If you give me seven-hundred-fifty words, I'll pay you a penny each. If it's good, I'll put the piece in a front page box above the fold and give you a by-line."

Aleck bolted from the chair. "I'll do it!"

Scrappy looked at a clock on the far wall. "The presses downstairs roll at one o'clock. You've got an hour."

Plopping before a typewriter, Aleck gleefully rubbed his hands together and muttered, "Whiteside is on the story!"

As the city room filled with the rat-a-tat-tat of two typewriters that seemed to be dueling, Johnny Groover dropped a nickel in the Roadhouse jukebox and pressed a button to select his favorite Tex Ritter record. By the time he was back at the bar, Tex was singing, *"Rye whiskey, rye whiskey, I cry; if I don't get rye whiskey, well I think I will die."*

Leaning with his back against the bar beside Minetta

and letting his eyes roam the room, Johnny said, "Billy Lee Austin and I used to sing this song sometimes. Old Billy Lee had a good voice. I sounded more like a frog in heat."

Minetta grinned. "What does a frog in heat sound like?"

"Me when I'm singing."

"If the ocean was whiskey and I was a duck, I'd dive to the bottom and never come up."

Johnny turned, picked up his empty glass, and wiggled it at the bartender. When he took the glass, Johnny said, "This time make it rye. Double."

Minetta said, "Don't you think you've had enough?"

Looking sidelong at Minetta, Johnny smiled, then threw an arm about Minetta's shoulder. "Good ol' Tex has put me in the mood for rye. Do you like cowboy movies, Lieutenant?"

"Who doesn't?"

Johnny's arm slipped away and to his side. "Who's your favorite cowboy?"

"Randolph Scott. Yours?"

The bartender brought the rye.

"You're listenin' to him."

"If whiskey don't kill me, I'll live till I die."

"Most people think Roy Rogers is better," Johnny continued. "Compared to Tex, I think Roy's a sissy. You'll never shee Tex Shritter wearin' fancy shirts wish fringes."

"I really think that rye should be your last drink, Johnny. You're starting to slur your words."

The record stopped and Johnny gazed longingly toward the Wurlitzer as a soldier stood before it. He chose Gene Autry's "Mexicali Rose."

"I'd play 'Rye Whiskey' again," Johnny said, raising his glass to his lips, "but that was my only nickel."

As Johnny gulped the rye, Minetta said, "Okay, Johnny, do you want to tell me what it is that's eating at you?"

"What makes you think shumthin's eatin' at me?"

"Ever since we've been traveling together, all the way from the Canal, you never drank this much. If it's because of that tin badge chief of police, forget about it. I can handle him."

"Thanks, but I dunt need no help. I know just what's he's gonna ask me about."

"Do you know what happened to the stickup money?"

"The last time I saw that dough was at the football field when we all split up. The plan was for all of us to lie low for a couple of weeks, then get together someplace safe to divvy it up. That's what I told to Chief Detwiler and it's what I'll tell him again, 'cause it's the truth."

"Who held on to the money?"

"That was Pete." He drained the rye. "What a double crosser he turned out to be. That was his plan all along, I suppose."

When he wiggled the empty glass toward the bartender, Minetta took it from his hand. "Last one, Johnny. Time for you to hit the sack. The bugle is sounding Lights Out."

"Says shoo? Says *who*?"

"These bars say," Minetta said, pointing to the symbols of rank on his collar." As he did so, the door opened and three soldiers with MP armbands came in. Assuming they were on duty, he whispered, "There's another reason for us to get outta here."

Johnny turned to look. "They don't look so tough."

"Maybe not, but there's three of them and they're sober."

"Okay, okay. I get your point."

As they passed them on their way toward the door, a corporal grasped Johnny's arm and exclaimed, "If it ain't the Marine hero! What's a fuckin' leatherneck doing in an Army bar?"

A metal name tag pinned to his brown jacket read GOR-DON.

Minetta seized the hand that held Johnny's arm and jerked it away. "Back off, mister."

Gordon sneered at Johnny. "What's he, your body guard?"

"What I am is an officer in the United States Navy whom you've neglected to address as 'Sir' and to salute," said Minetta, his voice rising over the music and the droning of the crowd as all eyes in the bar turned to him. "And if you want to avoid a whole lot of trouble, *Corporal,* you had better snap one off right now. And your buddies, too."

They did so smartly.

Returning the salutes, Minetta said, "And one more thing, Corporal Gordon. If you hope to get out of that uniform alive and in one piece, I advise you to never again address a Marine as a *fuckin'* leatherneck. You're lucky I'm here to keep this particular Marine—he's a sergeant, by the way—from handing you your head."

Red in the face and with jaw muscles twitching, Gordon blurted out, "All I got to say to you, *Sergeant,* is that as long as you're in town, you'd better stay away from my woman."

Johnny lurched toward him with clenched fists. "What the hell you talkin' about?"

"I'm talkin' about Pat Roberts."

"Point number one," said Johnny as Minetta stepped between him and Gordon, "it's been over between her and me for a long time. Point two, where I come from, decent men don't talk about their women in honky-tonks."

"That's enough," said Minetta, shoving Johnny toward the door. "We're out of here."

"Hey, Groover," yelled Gordon as they left. "The next time I run into you, I hope you're all by yourself."

27

USUALLY AN APPRENTICE pressman emerged from the bowels of the basement with copies of the *Independence* to drop onto Scrappy MacFarland's desk at half past one. But this morning he appeared an hour later. The last time there had been a press run this late, as best he could recall, was the night the paper had been held up for last-minute stories about the arrest of the maid for the murder of Amanda Burford Griffith.

"Ah ha, the moment of truth has arrived," exclaimed Scrappy to Aleck as the bundle of newspapers landed on his desk. Picking up the top one, he held it to his nose and sniffed. "I love the smell of fresh printer's ink!"

Aleck eagerly snatched a copy and found his article where Scrappy had promised to place it. Set off in a box on the front page above the fold, it was headlined:

A BOY COMES HOME A MAN

The essay began:

> In Ancient Rome when a general rode in his char-
> iot in triumphal procession through the streets, with
> the spoils of his conquest following in the form of
> strange beasts, the vanquished marching behind in
> chains, and wagons teeming with treasures, a slave
> stood behind him holding a wreath of laurels and re-
> peatedly whispering in his ear, "Remember, thou art
> only a man." Today, the heroes whom we laud are
> but boys. One of these, Sergeant John Groover of
> the United States Marine Corps, was hailed last
> night in a faux Moroccan night club. No celebration
> for a Caesar was more deserved. And no returning
> hero in the memory of this observer accepted his
> laurels with any more easy grace and captivating
> charm. Nobody had to remind him that he was but a
> mortal. Indeed, he had on his face an expression that
> pleaded, "This is all very nice, but golly, folks,
> you've made a terrible mistake."

Aleck put down his copy and shook his head ruefully. "For this excellent prose you are paying me a mere seven dollars and fifty cents?"

"Six and a quarter, Aleck," said Scrappy. "I counted your words." He looked up from his copy of the paper. "When you're done patting yourself on the back, let me know what you think of my story."

"I read it as you wrote it, remember?"

"Yeah, but it reads a lot better in twelve-point type."

The story was under the headline LARGE JOYOUS CROWD FETES OUR HERO.

"You're a superb journalist, Scrappy," Aleck said as he finished reading. "Shall I phone Western Union to send you a congratulatory wire?"

"You can congratulate me by buying me a big breakfast at the Vale-Rio Diner. It stays open all night."

"The town that never sleeps!"

"You say that mockingly, but you'll see that it's true," said Scrappy as they left the city room. "Before the war the town did roll up its sidewalks after the Colonial's last picture show. Not anymore. Now the steel plant and a few other factories are run twenty-four hours a day, so taverns that used to close at midnight stay open to the legal limit of four A.M., and the Vale-Rio serves breakfast round the clock. Because the war has people working seven days a week, stores that stayed open late only on Friday and Saturday nights find it worth their while to keep their doors open for shopping by people whose nights off are during the week. And a lot of folks who used to read the *Independence* at their breakfast tables peruse it with supper as if it were an evening newspaper."

"I stand corrected and chastened," said Aleck as they emerged from the building. "I shall never disdain the American small town again, even in jest."

When they arrived at the diner, they found its parking lot nearly filled and most seats at the counter and booths occupied by men and a few women wearing working clothes. The music on the jukebox was "When the Lights Go on Again All Over the World" by Vaughn Monroe.

As they settled into a corner booth, Scrappy whispered to Aleck, "The scrawny man in the bib overalls and painter's cap sitting at the far end of the counter is Delmer Turner."

Aleck peered at him and seemed puzzled for a moment, then softly exclaimed, "He's the payroll deliveryman that Johnny Groover and the gang stuck up! I'd no idea he was so elderly."

Scrappy continued in a whisper, "I'm surprised to see him here. He's usually at work at this time at the Graf moving and storage warehouse. He's the night watchman."

A waitress came to the booth. Flipping through her order book to a blank sheet, she said, "Will it be the usual scrapple and fried eggs, Mr. MacFarland?"

"Absolutely, darling."

"Just toast and coffee for me," said Aleck.

"We're outta butter, so it'll have to be oleo. Or would you prefer grape jelly?"

As Aleck pondered, Delmer Turner left the counter and gave a wave toward Scrappy.

"What about French toast?" Aleck asked the waitress.

"No problem, only it'll be made with oleo."

"That's fine," said Aleck as Delmer Turner strode toward the booth. "Can you bring my coffee now?"

"Mine too," said Scrappy.

"Sure thing," the waitress replied as Delmer arrived.

"Hello, Mr. MacFarland," he said. "Long time no see."

"How's it going, Delmer? Night off for you?"

"One of the fellas I worked his shift for is paying me back. Trouble is, I'm so used to being up all night, I couldn't get to sleep."

"This is Alexander Whiteside," said Scrappy with a nod toward Aleck. "You've heard his talks on the radio, I'm sure."

Delmer lifted his cap and scratched his head. "Can't say

that I have. No offense meant, mister. I keep my radio tuned to music."

Aleck smiled. "It's a free country, Mr. Turner."

The cap went back on. "Well, I just wanted to say hello, Mr. MacFarland. A pleasure to make your acquaintance, Mr. Whiteman."

"And the same to you, sir," said Aleck.

With Delmer gone, Scrappy said, "He's a sad figure, really. That robbery cost him his job with the courier firm. His boss held him responsible because he broke company rules by not keeping on driving and stopped to help the kid in the road with the bike."

"Proving once again that the road to hell is crowded with poor lost souls who made the mistake of having good intentions."

"By the way, did I ever tell you how much I've enjoyed you and your orchestra on the radio, Mr. Whiteman?"

"Since we keep coming back to the payroll robbery, I can't believe that Chief Detwiler believes that after all this time he can still lay his hands on the loot."

"It's not *finding* the money that he cares about. It's a matter of him closing the book on the case. He considers not accounting for the money a blot on his record as a policeman. Tom is a very proud man."

"Yet he wasn't too proud to accept Kate Fallon's help in murder cases."

"Yes, but Kate made sure that Tom and his police force got the credit."

"She is adamantly against granting me an interview on the subject of her detective work. I expect you to persuade her to change her mind."

"That's a fool's errand, my friend. You might as well

ask me to walk on water or say a magic word and change oleomargarine into butter."

Bringing their coffee, the waitress said, "Your food will be right out."

After taking a sip and surveying the customers seated at the counter, Aleck sighed and said, "Here I am in a diner in the very heart of America and I look at these simple, hardworking, patriotic men and women wishing I possessed the insights and talent to pick up a pen and write like Damon Runyon or wield a brush to paint in the style of a Norman Rockwell."

"Do you always wax this sentimental at three A.M.?"

"In the innermost part of a man's soul it is always three o'clock in the morning."

"Thank you F. Scott Fitzgerald."

"That poor bedeviled snob could never capture the essence of this tableau. John O'Hara tried in a few of his short stories and he almost got it in *Appointment in Samara*. Now, of course, he's too sophisticated, dazzled by the delights of the Big City and spoiled by too many nights in the barroom of the 21 Club. I suppose that means the definitive novel about the people of small-town America will have to be written by a keen observer of the species named MacFarland."

Scrappy shook his head. "There's not a literary bone in my body. I wouldn't even know how to begin writing a book. Besides, I have nothing to say. And no imagination."

The waitress brought their orders.

"One of the guests at my New Year's Eve party was the intrepid head of the New York Police Department, Lew Valentine," said Aleck, examining the French toast.

"Lew's certainly come a long way," Scrappy said as he drenched his scrapple in catsup. "He was so honest and stepped on so many toes that I never figured he'd ever get above the rank of captain. That he did says a lot about Mayor La Guardia."

"I'll pass that along to Fiorello."

"And tell Lew I think he's doing a great job as police commissioner."

"At my party I told Lew about the extraordinary numbers of crimes that have recently occurred in your little town."

"I'll bet he was fascinated."

"As I was thinking about it on the train on my way down here, I recalled an observation by Sherlock Holmes to Dr. Watson when they were on a case requiring them to venture out into the English countryside. The good doctor was prattling about the rolling hills, the little red and gray rooftops, and the beauties of the scenery. Holmes observed the same view from the train window and was horrified. He looked at that pastoral scene and in his mind envisioned the deeds of hellish cruelty and hidden wickedness going on year in and year out in such places and none the wiser. If that's not a subject for you to write about, I don't know what is. Good lord, man, to find your characters all you have to do is look around. For instance, the man who's lost his job because he allowed his heart to override his head by stopping to aid a kid who'd fallen off his bicycle in the middle of a country road. Not only did he find himself looking down the barrel of a gun, but two years later he finds that one of the gang who robbed him is hailed as a hero."

"I grant you that Delmer Turner is probably a bitter old

man," said Scrappy, lifting a fork with a mound of scrapple toward his mouth, "and I appreciate your confidence in yours truly as a potential winner of the Pulitzer Prize for literature, but I think I'll stick to everyday newspaper work and leave the novel writing to people who know what they're doing. There's also a paper shortage. I consider it my patriotic duty not to waste any of it on a manuscript that would have a snowball's chance in hell of getting published. Now eat your French toast before it gets cold so I can dump you at your hotel and go home to bed. You may be accustomed to sitting up till the crack of dawn talking with your literary friends and lamenting the state of the American novel, but I'm not. If there hadn't been a party for Johnny Groover, the paper would have been put to bed by ten o'clock and I would have been sawing wood six hours ago."

28

W HEN HARRY GROOVER'S alarm clock rang, he had
been lying awake in bed for over three hours. He'd
left the front door unlocked and a light on in the hallway
for Johnny and gone to bed as usual at nine. He'd wound
the bedside clock and checked to be certain it was set to
the right time. A little after one he found himself awak-
ened by the slam of a car door. When the car drove off,
he'd expected Johnny to come in and up the stairs. Instead, he heard him talking briefly to someone in front of
the house. They'd spoken too softly for him to understand
what they were saying, or even whether Johnny was talking to a man or a woman.

At one point in the conversation Johnny laughed and
said, "Ah, hell, why not?"

A car started up and went away, but Johnny didn't
come in.

Turning off the alarm, Harry got out of bed to get ready

for work. Dressed in his white milkman's uniform, he wondered if he might have fallen back to sleep for a while and during that time Johnny had come home quietly and gone to bed.

Looking into Johnny's room, Harry saw that he hadn't.

The bedroom was exactly as the day Johnny went off to the Marine Corps. A single bed was covered with a blue blanket with centered, overlapping letters N and D in gold, the symbol of Notre Dame University. Johnny had always dreamed of going there and playing football for the famous "Fighting Irish," even though he wasn't Irish and a Roman Catholic and didn't have high enough grades in school to get in. The emblem had been sewn on the blanket by Johnny's mother. She'd cut it from one of two Notre Dame pennants that Coach Franklin brought home for Johnny from a Notre Dame–Perdue game the coach had attended in South Bend. The second banner was tacked to the wall above a bureau opposite the foot of the bed so that it would be the first thing Johnny saw when he woke up. Surrounding it were framed photographs of Johnny in the uniforms he'd worn playing for the Memorial Junior High School Rebels and the senior high Phantoms. Six were photographs of his teams, grades seven through twelve. A large picture that had been in the *Independence* was of Johnny being presented the county league's most valuable player trophy by Scrappy MacFarland at the end of Johnny's last season. In several smaller ones he was snapped in action racing along the sideline, lunging across a goal line for a touchdown, and with right arm raised for a pass. In two frames he was with Richie Zale and Pete Slattery, each with a serious expression. In a third Johnny and Richie were wearing dirt-smudged jerseys, grinning, and with an arm around one another's waist.

In a corner of the bedroom was a full duffle bag with Johnny's name and Marine Corps identification number stenciled in black on one side. Next to it were shiny black shoes to go with the dress uniform and stiff round hat hanging neatly from a hook on the closet door. Looking at it, Harry could almost hear Johnny's mother of blessed memory yelling at him as she picked up his clothing from where he'd left them in heaps when Johnny was growing up. The least Johnny could do, Hannah had told him again and again, was to take care of the things his father worked so hard for, getting up in the middle of the night to deliver milk, so Johnny would have decent things to wear when he went to school and on Saturday nights to the movies.

Then she'd throw up her hands and say, "I pity any girl that marries you. She'll spend all her time cleaning up after you."

Johnny certainly had a lot of girlfriends. With a little smile Harry recalled the day when he was rummaging through his bureau drawer looking for something or other and discovered that instead of six prophylactics he kept in it, there were only five. When Johnny came home from football practice that day, he'd stopped him on his way upstairs to his room and asked, "Johnny, is there anything you need to talk to me about?"

Johnny's face flushed as he stammered, "T-talk to you a-about? Like, uh, what?"

"Man stuff? Girls? You can talk to me, you know."

"Don't worry, Pop," Johnny said, heading up the steps two at a time. "I've known all about the birds and the bees for a couple of years now."

"Oh? Who've you been talking to?"

"Come on, Pop. This is kind of embarrassing."

"Not everything that you might hear from other boys is correct."

"Relax, Pop," Johnny said, going into his room and closing the door. "Coach Franklin talks about all that in hygiene class."

A picture of the girl Harry hoped Johnny would marry, pretty Millie Parker, stood atop the bureau. But after Johnny got into trouble and had to go into the Marines to keep from going to jail, Millie had married Richie Zale.

Turning from the doorway of his grown-up son's room, Harry wondered what Hannah would say if she could come back from the grave and see how neat the room was. Going downstairs, he thought she would probably say something like, "Well, thank the Good Lord for miracles and hooray for the United States Marine Corps."

Going into the kitchen, he supposed that if Hannah had lived to see Johnny being praised as a hero, the tears of pride would be flowing like the water in the Schuylkill River. Seated at the table eating a small bowl of corn flakes, he was glad that she'd not lived to see her beloved baby standing in front of Judge Wooten and admitting that he was a highway robber.

"It's those Perillo boys that got Johnny in trouble," Harry could hear Hannah saying as clearly as if she were standing by the stove. "And that Pete Slattery, too. I always said that one was a rotten apple. What Johnny found to like in him was beyond my understanding."

"What Johnny saw in Pete Slattery," Harry would say to her if she could hear him now, "was what young boys who want to play football always find in older ones who are the stars they dream of being one day."

Finished with the cereal, Harry took the bowl and spoon to the sink and left them there as if Hannah would wash them and put them away, as she'd done for nearly forty years.

Leaving the house, he thought he heard her say, "Remember to bring home three quarts of milk. We're all out."

As he took out a ring of keys to bolt the front door, he remembered that Johnny wasn't home yet and left it unlocked. Walking to the corner, he arrived just as the bus he took to work pulled in. When he got on, Bill Taylor, the driver, said, "What are you doing going to work today, Harry? I thought you'd be taking a few days off and spending them with Johnny."

Harry smiled. "We're short-handed at the dairy."

"Say, Harry," said Steve Padula, the only other passenger, "that was some parade they had for Johnny the other day, wasn't it?"

Harry took his customary seat at the back of the bus and wondered where Johnny could have spent the night.

29

As the Lockheed P-38 Lightning swooped down on a line of Panzer tanks in the Tunisian desert, First Lieutenant Paul Fallon could not understand why the voice of his squadron leader in the earphones of his leather flying helmet sounded just like his mother.

"If you're not down here in two minutes," the voice commanded, "I'm coming up and dragging you out of that bed by the scruff of your neck."

Waking up before he could see if the bombs he'd dropped had knocked out the target he had in his sights, Paulie wanted to go back to sleep and finish the dream.

But now it was his sister Kate's voice coming from the hallway.

"Time to rise and shine, little brother."

When he entered the kitchen carrying gym clothes and sneakers wrapped in a towel, his mother was standing by the stove and Kate was at the table eating oatmeal.

As he set the bundle on a chair, Kate said, "It's gym day, I see. Coach Franklin was up late last night at the party, so maybe he'll go easy on everyone today."

The Philco radio on the counter was tuned to news, but not about the war.

The announcer was talking about three people who were killed in a big fire during the night in Philadelphia.

"What a terrible way to die," said Kate as Paulie sat opposite her.

Mrs. Fallon set a bowl of oatmeal in front of him.

"Go easy on the sugar, boy," she said. "Mr. Tynan at the A&P says he doesn't know when he'll be getting more in, and we're down to our last pound."

"I don't see what sugar has to do with winning the war," Paulie said, sprinkling the oatmeal with one teaspoonful instead of two.

"Neither do I," said Mrs. Fallon, "but that's the way it is, so there's no use complaining."

"How was the big party, Kate?" Paulie asked.

"Very nice," she answered. "Everybody seemed to have a good time. The only sour note came near the end when Chief Detwiler made a perfect jerk of himself. I was so mad at him I felt like slapping his face."

With a mouthful of oatmeal, Paulie asked, "What did he do that was so bad?"

Mrs. Fallon smacked the back of his head. "How many times do I have to tell you not to talk and eat at the same time?"

"He told Johnny—no, he *ordered* him—to be at police headquarters this morning to be questioned again about the robbery. It was an outrageous thing to do. Absolutely the wrong time and place for it!"

The man on the radio said, "And now the weather outlook. Increasing cloudiness today with temperatures in the low thirties. Snow is expected to begin late this afternoon and continue into the morning, possibly heavy at times."

"Great," Paulie exclaimed. "Maybe we won't have school tomorrow."

"Well, you have it today," said Mrs. Fallon, "so finish your breakfast and get a move on or you'll be late getting there."

"On gym days I don't have homeroom. I go right to the gym. So even if I was late a couple of minutes, it doesn't matter. Mr. Franklin hardly ever takes attendance."

"Even if I *were* late," said Kate, "it *wouldn't* matter."

"Anyway, on Thursdays we don't go to the gym," Paulie continued. "We go right to the football field and spend the hour running around the track, except the ones on the football team. They have to practice blocking and running new plays that Mr. Franklin thought up and wants to try out for next season. He keeps talking about what a good player Jack Fallon was and asking me if I'm going to follow in my big brother's footsteps and go out for football. He puts his arm around my shoulders and says, 'You've got the build of a halfback.'"

"Are you going to try for the team?" Kate asked. "You'd make Dad happy if you did."

"I was thinking of seeing if I can get on the school newspaper. Miss Thomas says if I do and work hard, I could probably be the editor next year."

"Can't you do both?"

"Not really."

The radio announcer said, "And that's the news of the

hour. Now stay tuned for music on 'The Morning Show' with your host Jim Kershner."

"Maybe someday I'll read the news on the radio," said Paulie.

"Well, whatever you do, I know you'll make us all proud of you," said Kate. Looking at the wall clock, she exclaimed, "Gosh, look at the time. I'd better get going or I'll miss my bus."

"Better take your umbrella," said Mrs. Fallon. "The radio calls for snow when you'll be coming home."

"Come on, Paulie, get your coat on," Kate said. "You can walk me to the bus stop."

"I'm goin' the other way today," he said, grabbing his gym clothes. "I'm walkin' to school with Al Liebholz. I'm meetin' him over at his house."

"Okay, but if you're going to be giving the news on the radio," said Kate, putting on her coat as she headed for the door, "you'd better learn not to drop your g's when you speak."

As Paulie hurriedly finished the oatmeal, Jim Kershner was saying, "Welcome to 'The Morning Show.' To get everyone in the mood for the snow that's coming our way, here's Tommy Dorsey and his orchestra with their 1941 hit recording of 'Winter Weather.'"

Five minutes later Al Liebholz bounded down the steps of his house. Paulie greeted him with an anxious look and blurted out, "Did you get them?"

"Of course I got them," said Al, plunging a hand into a pocket of his overcoat. "One for you, me, and Ronnie, if he shows up."

From the pocket came the hand and three cigarettes.

"What kind?" asked Paulie excitedly.

"Lucky Strikes."

"Are you sure your old man isn't goin' to miss 'em?"

"I've been sneaking them from different packs, one at a time."

"What about matches?"

The hand went into the pocket and came out with a book with a large V for victory on the back. "He leaves these all over the house. There's eight left in this one."

The plan was to meet Ronnie Smith at the Washington Field gate farthest from the field house and smoke the cigarettes behind the old grandstand. But as Al had feared, Ronnie was not there at the agreed time.

"I knew Ronnie would turn sissy on us," said Al in disgust.

Paulie said, "Maybe we should give him a couple more minutes."

"Hell no," said Al, pushing open the gate.

Following him, Paulie said nervously, "We could do this another time."

Al stopped short. "Don't tell me you're getting cold feet all of a sudden!"

"Course not."

"Okay, then, follow me," said Al, breaking into a run.

Getting from the gate to the grandstand meant crossing the gridiron at midfield.

Running after Al, Paulie looked ahead to what appeared to be a bundle of brown rags at the fifty-yard line. But when he jogged past it, he saw that the rags were a man in a uniform. Stopping for a closer look at what he now supposed was a passed-out drunk, he cried out, "Oh Holy Christmas. I think this guy is Johnny Groover."

Bending over the motionless figure, Al muttered, "It's him all right."

"I guess he had too much to drink, huh?"

Al gave the figure a nudge with a foot, stepped back with a horrified look in his face, and said, "He ain't drunk, Paulie. He's . . . dead."

A Wallop in the
Solar Plexus

WITH EYES WIDE open and gaping jaw, I sat momentarily breathless at the edge of Scrappy MacFarland's bed, feeling as though he'd given me a wallop in the solar plexus.

"Wait just a second, Scrappy," I blurted out. "Are you telling me Johnny Groover's body was found by Paul Fallon?"

"Now you know why Paulie's been fixated on this for almost fifty years. I guess when you're a kid that age, discovering a corpse can be pretty unsettling."

"Traumatizing, I'd say."

"I probably didn't help Paulie much," said Scrappy with a chuckle, "when I told him that it's a general rule of the police that whoever reports finding someone dead in what looks like a murder most likely committed it."

"You didn't!"

"It seemed funny to me at the time."

"Geez, it's no wonder Paul's had this on his mind all these years."

"I think it wasn't finding Groover dead that stuck in his mind," he replied, "as much as the fact that he knew Johnny Groover had been murdered and that everybody else who knew it agreed to tell the public he'd died suddenly of complications from his war wounds."

"My god, Scrappy, how could you go along with that? You had an obligation to report the truth."

"As Pontius Pilate once asked a fellow named Jesus of Nazareth, 'What is truth?'"

"The ugly *truth* is that you knew he was murdered and you conspired to keep it quiet."

"Conspired?" He sat for a moment, thinking. "Yes, there's no other word for it. It was a conspiracy, pure and simple." He smiled. "Or is that an oxymoron?"

"I can do without the wisecracks, thank you."

"Before you go riding off on your high horse, kid, let me quote Winston Churchill. I'm paraphrasing him only slightly. He explained that the Allies set up a program of deception aimed at Germany that also included not leveling with the British and American people because sometimes the truth must be surrounded by a bodyguard of lies."

"Well, I'm glad that at long last you've decided the time's come to set the record straight about what happened to Johnny Groover."

"I'm telling you what happened. What you do with the information is up to you. Now please afford me the courtesy of reserving judgment on me and people who are not around to defend themselves until you've heard the whole story. Everything that we did that night and in the days following we all saw as our patriotic duty."

His eyes took on a faraway look, as though he were again standing on that fifty-yard line.

"Paulie and his friend ran like bats out of hell for the field house to tell Franklin what they'd found. Right away, Franklin grabbed the phone on his desk and told the policeman who answered that Johnny had been murdered. That set off a string of events that would not exactly have pleased Tom Detwiler. Under standing orders, the officer who took Franklin's call placed two phone calls. The first was to Detwiler's home, the second to Ed Polansky, the undertaker who had a contract with the county to act as coroner. Then, in an arrangement that I had with the overnight desk officer at headquarters, unbeknownst to Tom Detwiler, of course, my phone was the third one to ring. I immediately placed a call to the General Washington. I got the operator to connect me with both Aleck Whiteside and Lieutenant Minetta."

30

"**H**OW CAN THAT be?" Minetta exclaimed. "After the party we went to a bar and after that I dropped him at his home. That was around half past midnight. What the hell was he doing on a freaking football field in the middle of the night?"

"Whatever the reason," Scrappy replied, "it's an awkward situation."

"Yes, I take your point," said Aleck. "I can see the banner headline already: WAR HERO MURDERED ON THE NIGHT OF HIS HOMECOMING. And God only knows what Dr. Goebbels and his Nazi propaganda will make of this. Not to mention the howls of glee we'll hear from Japan."

"That's why I'm picking you two up at your hotel in ten minutes," said Scrappy. "We've got to talk Detwiler and the coroner into clamping a lid on this until we find out what happened. Once we've got our ducks in row, we may find a way to present a plausible explanation that will prevent the national press from descending on this town like vultures."

"The coroner could announce that Johnny died of complications arising from his war wounds," said Minetta. "He can say that Johnny suddenly collapsed at home. Nobody will have to know where this happened, or that he was murdered."

"Excuse me, gentlemen," said Aleck, "but if Johnny was murdered, the police can't overlook that fact and let whoever did it walk away. Once the killer is arrested, he'll have a right to a trial. If that happens, the cat's out of the bag in spades."

"One problem at a time, guys," said Scrappy. "First we get everyone marching in step."

When Mrs. Detwiler answered the telephone in the bedroom, her husband was shaving in the bathroom. "Tom, it's for you," she shouted. "It's Mickey Ludlum."

Observing her husband take the call in an undershirt tightly stretched by a bulging belly, brown trousers with yellow suspenders hanging over his behind, and his ruddy face half shaved and half thickly lathered, Mrs. Detwiler thought that he looked like W. C. Fields.

"No shit!" he said into the phone. "Are you sure you heard right?"

"There's no mistake, Chief," said Ludlum.

"The body was found where by who?"

"Two school kids spotted it at Washington Field. It's lying on the fifty-yard line. Coach Franklin called from his office in the field house."

"Okay. Get Todd Doebling and tell him to head out

there on the double. I'm on my way. Oh, did you call Ed Polansky?"

"I'm phoning him next."

"Good. You stand by. I'll probably need you to round up the guys on the day shift."

As he hung up, his wife asked, "What is it?"

"Somebody killed the Groover kid."

Mrs. Detwiler pressed a hand to her chest. "Oh my word!"

Hurrying back to the bathroom, Detwiler muttered, "Who says there's no justice?"

Nancy Roberts entered her sister's bedroom and found Pat in her slip and seated at her bureau combing her hair. "I heard you sneaking out in the middle of the night," Nancy said. "Where did you go?"

"I couldn't sleep, so I went out for a walk. I did not *sneak*."

Nancy sat on Pat's unmade bed. "Did you see Johnny Groover?"

Pat stopped combing. "Now where would I have seen him?"

"At the party!"

"Oh, yes, at the party," said Pat, resuming the combing. "Yeah, I saw him, but only for about a minute."

"Did you ask him if he got your letter?"

"We talked about it . . . briefly."

"Was he absolutely *crushed* by it?"

"Actually, he told me he took the news very well."

"Is he still cute?"

"He looked fine. I think he's put on a little weight."

"When's your next date with your soldier boy?"

"Saturday night. Dinner and a movie. Now, Miss Louella Parsons, please go away and let me get dressed in peace."

A sign on the wall had a glowering picture of Uncle Sam above the words:

TAKE WHAT YOU WANT
BUT EAT ALL YOU TAKE

Holding a tray and standing behind Corporal Bobby Gordon in the breakfast chow line in the cadre mess hall of George Washington Hospital, PFC Warren Baker said, "Man, am I hungover this morning!"

"The way you were knockin' back boiler makers at the Roundhouse," said Bobby as he held out a tray to a cook in a greasy white apron and sagging chef's hat behind the steam table, "it's no wonder you're hung."

The cook slapped a glob of creamed beef atop a slice of toast.

"You weren't doing so bad either after your retreat from your go-round with that Marine and Navy officer," said Baker. "Then I looked up and you were gone. Where'd you go running off to, downtown to cry on some dame's shoulder at Annie's whorehouse?"

Glaring at the cook, Bobby said, "Shit on a single again?"

"Life's a bitch," snapped the cook. "And then you marry her and get killed in action and she moves to Florida and lives happily ever after on your GI insurance. Move along, Corporal. I got an army to feed."

• • •

Richie Zale woke up on the parlor couch, went into the kitchen, and found Millie with her back to the door. Standing at the stove, she was warming a small pan of milk for the baby.

He knew he was in for it from her, or that he'd be getting the silent treatment, by cereal and sugar bowls, a spoon, a half-pint bottle of milk, and a box of Post Toasties on the table. When she wasn't mad at him, she cooked something. An empty cup was a mute signal that if he wanted coffee, he could help himself from the pot on the stove.

As he sat at the table, she spoke without turning around. "I thought you said you would be home at two o'clock."

"I had to work a little longer."

"Don't take me for a fool, Richie. Your breath was stinking of booze. I smelled it when I bent down by the couch to pick up your clothes where you dropped them."

"All right. I stopped at Toots's tavern after work for a couple of drinks."

She turned around. "With your bosom buddy?"

Richie shot to his feet and stormed from the kitchen. "I was *not* with Johnny Groover."

Because of a late-night phone call from Arthur Frick informing him that Arthur's father, Morris, had finally passed away from the cancer that had spread throughout Morris's body, Ed Polansky hadn't gotten to bed until after three o'clock. Awake at seven, he expected to spend the morning performing a routine autopsy and part of the afternoon consulting with Arthur about funeral arrangements. But all that would have to wait while he went out to Washington Field to provide a preliminary opinion on whether the young man who was found dead there was, in fact, the victim of a homicide.

The youth's identity, if he was Johnny Groover, had come as quite a shock. A few hours earlier when Ed and his wife had seen him at the welcome-home reception at the junior high school, Johnny had looked in the pink of health, except for a slight right-leg limp. Still, he had read that Groover had suffered several bullet wounds, one of them to the chest. It was possible that an old blood clot in a lung had broken loose and traveled to his heart or his brain, resulting in sudden death.

31

WHEN TODD DOEBLING arrived at Washington Field, he found the chief of police's car in front of the field house. As he entered, two boys were seated on benches in the locker room. He asked them, "Where's Chief Detwiler?"

Paulie Fallon pointed to a closed door and said, "In Coach Franklin's office."

As he entered, Detwiler was telling Coach Franklin, "I want you to keep the kids in your class away from the football field, except for the two who found the body."

"No problem, Chief," said Franklin. "I've sent everyone but Paul and Al Leibholz to their homerooms."

"What did you tell them?"

"I said that there's a man drunk on the football field."

"That's good. But I expect you to keep your mouth shut about this until I've found out what happened here. For now, you remain here. I want the kids who found the body to take me to it and tell me what they saw and did."

"They ran in here and told me that Johnny Groover was dead. They were terrified. I'm the one who called your office and reported the murder. This is just . . . horrible."

Stepping from the office, Detwiler wiggled a finger at the boys. "I need you to show me and Officer Doebling the body. Don't be scared, okay?"

As they left the field house, Ed Polansky's big black Cadillac pulled up. Getting out with a black leather valise in hand, he asked, "Is it really Johnny Groover?"

Ronnie answered, "It's him all right."

"I thought it was a pile of rags," said Paulie. "But then we saw it was a man. He looked to me like a drunk. Then Ronnie looked at his face and told me that it was Johnny Groover and that he was dead."

Detwiler asked, "Did either of you touch anything?"

"Not me," said Ronnie.

"Me neither," Paulie said. "We just ran to tell Mr. Franklin."

"You did good, boys," Detwiler said as they went around the field house.

A few moments later, kneeling by the corpse, Polanksy said, "Blow to the back of the head with a heavy object. Very little blood. Death would have been almost instantaneous."

"Check his pockets, Todd," said Doebling. "It could have been a robbery."

"Who pulls a holdup on the fifty-yard line of a football field in the middle of the night?"

"Just check the damn pockets, okay?" As he spoke, he saw three men striding toward the gridiron from the direction of the field house. "Oh shit, it's Scrappy MacFarland, that friend of his from New York, and that Navy officer."

Scrappy arrived, followed by Minetta. Aleck lagged a little behind them, breathing hard.

Detwiler demanded, "How the hell did you find out about this, MacFarland?"

"Glenda the Good Witch of the North wafted through my window in her pink balloon and told me to get my ass out to Washington Field."

Dewtiler glared at Polansky.

"Hey, wait a minute," said the funeral director. "He didn't get it from me."

Finished with the pockets, Doebling said, "He's got his wallet on him and ten bucks, so it doesn't look like robbery, Chief."

"How I found out about this is not the point," Scrappy said. "What's important is how this thing is going to be handled."

"It will be handled in the usual way," Detwiler said, "and as chief of police I am telling you and your pals to get yourselves away from this crime scene. Unless you want to be arrested on a charge of impeding an investigation, scram. Now!"

"No one's interested in interfering with your investigation, Tom. But I don't think you've considered the ramifications of what you've got on your hands."

"What I've got is a murder. Butt out, Scrappy."

Aleck exclaimed indignantly, "Butt out of the murder of a *war hero*?"

"Look, Mr. Big Shot from New York," said Detwiler, "in this town a murder is a murder and it's going to be treated in the ordinary way no matter what *implications* there might be."

"According to my information," Aleck retorted, "your ordinary way of solving a murder is to turn it over to a certain young woman."

"Oh, that's cute."

"Gentlemen, gentlemen, this squabbling is getting us nowhere," implored Lieutenant Minetta. "The implications that we're asking you to consider, Chief Detwiler, are of the gravest nature in terms of how this tragedy is to be perceived, not just in Robinsville but nationally and all over the world. If this isn't handled in the right way—"

"What are you saying, Mr. Navy Man," Detwiler growled, "that I'm a bungling nincompoop who doesn't know his ass from a hole in the ground? May I point out that you're the person who was supposed to be baby-sitting Groover? It seems to me that you bear some responsibility for what happened. Where were you last night?"

"After the party Johnny wanted to have a drink. We went to a hillbilly bar called the Roadhouse. When I dropped Johnny off at his home around one o'clock, I assumed he would be going right to bed because he was seeing you in the morning."

"Nobody's accusing you of being incapable, Tom," said Scrappy. "What we're saying is that there are vital issues that you must take into consideration before you proceed any further in this matter."

"First it's implications," said Detwiler. "Now it's *vital issues*. Such as what?"

"If this situation is handled in the ordinary way," Scrappy replied, "you're going to end up feeling like a high-wire walker in the Barnum and Bailey Circus. Once word gets out across the country that a war hero has been murdered in his hometown, the national press will swarm all over the place like flies on a manure pile. Unless this is handled right, we'll have egg on our faces, believe me. Robinsville will become a laughingstock."

"And so will the country," said Aleck grimly, "all over the globe."

"I can't just sweep this under the rug, for crissakes."

"Of course you can't, and no one's asking you to."

"Just what are you asking?"

"For a little time is all."

"I'm listening."

Scrappy turned to Polansky. "Ed, have you determined the cause of death?"

Polansky looked at Detwiler. "Chief?"

"He'll find out sooner or later, so go ahead and tell him."

"He appears to have died from a crushing blow with a heavy object at the back of the head, probably around two o'clock this morning. I'm confident that's what I'll find at autopsy."

"But you can't say *officially* until you've done the autopsy?"

"Yes, but I'd be surprised if that wasn't the cause."

"How long does an autopsy usually take?"

"In this instance it shouldn't be more than an hour."

Scrappy glanced at Lieutenant Minetta, then said to Polansky, "Suppose you received an order from someone in Washington to hold off on the autopsy until someone came to observe the autopsy from, say, the Navy Department?"

Polansky smiled slyly. "I'd hold off till he got here."

"In the meantime," said Scrappy, "you would not be in a position to inform Tom that he had a murder to investigate?"

"That's right. A death without a witness or witnesses cannot be officially classified as a homicide without my say-so."

"But in that same meantime may I point out," objected Detwiler, "that Groover's killer could be making his getaway."

"Your point is well taken, Tom," said Scrappy. "Do you have a suspect?"

"Come on, Scrappy. The investigation's just started."

Scrappy's eyes turned toward Paulie Fallon. "What about Paulie? Isn't it a police theory that whoever reports finding a murder victim probably did it?"

Looking terrified, Paulie shouted, "I was home in bed at two o'clock."

"Me too," Al blurted out.

Scrappy chuckled. "Is there someone who can vouch for your alibi, Paulie?"

"My mom can. And my sisters Kate and Arlene. Dad can't because he was at work."

"Enough of this kidding around, Scrappy," said Detwiler. "What are you getting at with all this stuff about Ed holding off on conducting the autopsy?"

"I'm asking you to let us have a little time."

"Us? Who's us?"

"Us is yourself, me, Aleck, Lieutenant Minetta, and maybe Kate Fallon."

"Now just a damn minute. I won't have you dragging her in on this."

"Most murders involve people who know one another. Would you agree that whoever killed Johnny Groover was most likely an acquaintance, even a friend? Kate knows all of them."

"I can think of a couple of people who weren't his friends who could have done this. There's that Perillo woman. She blamed Groover for getting her three sons mixed up in the payroll robbery."

"Mrs. Perillo couldn't have done it. She's under observation in a mental hospital."

"I forgot about that. Okay, how about the delivery man, Delmer Turner?"

"He's a real possibility," Aleck interjected. "He was out and about. We saw him at the Vale-Rio Diner."

"What's that?" asked Detwiler excitedly.

"Aleck and I had the pleasure of talking briefly with Turner," Scrappy answered. "That was about what time, Aleck?"

"Around three o'clock," said Aleck. "If Johnny was killed at approximately two o'clock, he could have done it."

"True, but did he strike you as looking like someone who'd just committed a murder?"

"I once covered a case in which the killer, a woman, had slit her husband's throat in the parlor and went into the kitchen and fixed herself dinner."

Detwiler turned to Officer Doebling. "Todd, run out to Turner's place and bring him in. I'll question him when I'm done here."

"Excuse me, Tom," said Scrappy, "but I think that's not what you should be doing right now. If you haul Delmer in, there's no way we can keep a lid on this."

"Screw keeping a lid on," said Doebling. "He could be skipping out as we speak!"

"Where would he skip to?"

"Who the hell knows?"

"Think about it, Todd. If you were Johnny Groover, would you be standing in the middle of this football field in the middle of the night with the man you'd helped rob, and who holds you responsible for humiliating him and costing him his job? No, Johnny wasn't here at two in the morning with Delmer Tuner. He was here with someone he trusted. A friend."

Doebling looked anxiously at Detwiler. "Do I pick up Delmer or not?"

The chief of police gazed at the body and scratched his jaw. "No. Scrappy's right. Turner probably didn't do this. And if he did, he's not going anywhere."

Impatiently, Doebling asked, "So we just sit on our asses?"

Minetta said, "There's one person whose whereabouts you could check out."

"Oh? Who's that?" asked Detwiler.

"He's an MP corporal at the Army hospital, name of Gordon. He and Johnny almost had a fight at the Road-house."

"Over what?"

"The subject was a woman. Apparently Gordon is involved with one of Johnny's former girlfriends. I had to step in to keep them from going at it."

"I think this corporal killing Johnny is a longshot for the same reason I think we can rule out Delmer Turner," said Scrappy. "It's obvious that after Lieutenant Minetta left Johnny at his home around one o'clock, Johnny didn't go to bed, but went out again. Why? To settle things with Gordon? That doesn't make sense. How would Gordon know where Johnny was staying? And even if Gordon knew and showed up at the house, why would they come all the way out here to take care of business? I come back to my point that Johnny came here with someone he knew and trusted."

Detwiler sighed. "Okay, Mr. Buttinski, what's your idea?"

"There's no reason for Ed to delay the autopsy, since it's pretty obvious what the cause of death was. But as far as what the public is told about this, I'll run a story in tomorrow's paper that the cause of Johnny's death is undetermined, pending an autopsy, which Ed has put off until the arrival of observers from Washington."

"You can print that it's possible Johnny died as the result of complications from his wounds," said Polansky. "You can say that the complication might have been an old blood clot. It could have become dislodged, resulting in a heart attack or a fatal stroke."

"That will buy us time for a discreet investigation of Johnny's friends," said Scrappy with an emphatic nod. "Which is where Kate Fallon enters the picture, if she's willing."

"What's the explanation for her going around and asking questions?" said Detwiler.

Scrappy frowned and thought for a moment, then startled Aleck by clapping a hand on Aleck's shoulder. "Kate will be assisting Aleck in preparing a script for his radio show on the subject of Johnny's life. Kate is helping Aleck find friends of Johnny's to interview."

"That's brilliant," exclaimed Aleck. "I'll title it 'Salute to a Hero.' "

"While that's going on, Tom," Scrappy said, "you can discreetly check out Delmer and the corporal."

"I'll let you have two days. If you're at a dead end at that time, I turn my men loose."

"We'll get started right away."

Minetta said, "First, I've got to report this to Washington."

"Aleck and I will drop you at the hotel and pick you up after we talk to Kate."

"Since you're running a taxi service," said Detwiler, looking at the boys who found the body, "I don't think it's a good idea for them to be in school today. I'd appreciate it, Scrappy, if you'd take them home." To the boys he said, "I want you fellas to give me your word that you won't talk about what you've heard us saying. Do I have your pledge? Boy Scout's honor?"

Scared, solemn and together, they said, "Yes, sir."

As Scrappy, Aleck, Minetta, and the two boys walked to Scrappy's car, Aleck rubbed his hands together and declared, "Oh goody! Nancy Drew and Bulldog Drummond are on the case."

After leaving Minetta at the hotel and the two boys at their homes with admonitions from Scrappy to remember their Scout oaths to Chief Detwiler, Scrappy turned his Plymouth into the driveway of the Manyon's Precision Metals Company. Looking ahead to the long, low red brick building, Aleck said, "So this is where Kate Fallon is doing her bit for the war effort."

"She's a welder."

"Wonderful!"

A man in a guard's uniform at the reception desk asked, "May I help you?"

"Please tell Mr. Manyon that we need to see him," said Scrappy.

"Your names, please?"

"Just tell him Scrappy MacFarland is in the lobby."

The guard perked up. "The newspaper editor?"

"That's right."

Tall, slender, with white hair, Manyon appeared a few moments later. "Scrappy, this is a pleasant surprise."

Scrappy introduced Aleck.

"I never miss your Sunday radio programs, Mr. Whiteside," said Manyon. "What may I do for you gentlemen?"

"We need to talk with Kate Fallon," said Scrappy. "May we use your office?"

"Certainly. I hope there's no problem in Kate's family."

"Everything's fine on that front."

Manyon spoke to the guard. "Please use the PA system in the welding shop and ask Miss Fallon to come to my office."

She arrived wearing her coveralls and looking alarmed. "Scrappy! Aleck! What is it?"

"It's not about your folks," said Scrappy. "But it is bad news."

"We've come to ask your help in dealing with it," said Aleck.

"Have a chair, Kate," Scrappy said, "and I'll put you in the picture."

Except to gasp "Oh no" when he told her of Johnny Groover's murder, she sat quietly and listened intently while Scrappy related everything they knew and explained their purpose.

At the conclusion of the narrative, she sat thinking for several moments, then squared her shoulders and said, "There's a crucial point I have to be clear about. Are you quite certain when Coach Franklin reported the finding of Johnny's body on the football field to the police that he didn't just say that Johnny Groover was dead? You're sure he said he'd been murdered?"

"I'm positive that's what Mickey Ludlum told me Franklin told him."

"Had Franklin actually seen Johnny's body?"

"*That* I can't say."

"Where's my brother at the moment?"

"We dropped him at your house on our way to see you."

Kate picked up the telephone and dialed her home. Her mother answered.

"Mom, is Paulie there?"

Mrs. Fallon asked, "Why isn't he in school?"

"Please put him on, Mom."

She shouted, "Paulie, Kate wants to talk to you."

When he came on the line, he whispered, "Did you solve the murder yet?"

Kate heard her mother in the background. "What murder?"

"Paulie, this is very important," said Kate. "After you told Mr. Franklin what you found on the football field, did he go out and look?"

"Look at what?"

"At the body!"

"Oh. Not right away."

"When did he look at it?"

"I think it was after the police came."

"You *think* or you *know*?"

Paulie paused. "He went out after the police got there. We all went out."

"Thanks, Paulie. How are you doing?"

"I'm doin' good. Why shouldn't I?"

"Well, you did find a dead body after all."

"Yeah, wasn't that neat? Was he really murdered?"

Mrs. Fallon exclaimed, "Who was murdered?"

"Tell Mom not to get worked up," Kate said. "I'll explain everything when I get home."

She hung up the phone.

"Well?" asked Scrappy eagerly.

"Coach Franklin did *not* go out to the football field and look at Johnny's body before he called the police."

Aleck lurched to his feet. "Of course! If he hadn't seen the body, how could he know that Johnny had been murdered? Kate, you are a genius."

On the Horns of
a Dilemma

"JEFFERSON, YOU LOOK as white as a bed sheet," said Scrappy MacFarland. "Shall I summon an attendant?"

"So it was the football coach who killed Johnny Groover," I blurted out. "Why did he do it?"

"The motive sure knocked the wind out of me."

Exasperated, I almost flew off the bed as I demanded, "Come on, Scrappy, quit beating around the bush. Cut to the chase."

With a shrug, he replied, "Franklin was afraid Johnny Groover was finally going to spill the beans about that payroll heist."

"Whoa! Are you saying Franklin had something to do with the robbery?"

"You could say he was an accomplice, but only after the fact."

I started pacing the room. "This is fantastic!"

"You could've knocked me over with a feather when I

heard it. But as Sherlock Holmes is famous for saying, 'When you have eliminated the impossible, whatever remains, however improbable, must be the truth.' "

I returned to the bed. "Take me through it step by step."

"I should have made the connection myself, of course. All the boys who pulled off that caper either were football players at the time, or in Pete Slattery's case, had been on the team. I chalked that fact up to coincidence, like everybody else did at the time. I also concluded that it was Pete Slattery who'd tipped the cops to the identity of the robbers. But he couldn't have been the one because he was dead."

"Scrappy, if you're stringing me along about this!"

He jerked in his chair as if I'd slapped his face. "Why would I do such a thing?"

"Maybe you're just an old and lonely man enjoying the pleasure of my company."

"An old man I am, and lonely sometimes, but I've gotten used to both. Take my advice, young man. Don't ever become a senior citizen!"

"That remark was out of line. I apologize."

"And never apologize. Your friends don't need it and your enemies won't believe you."

"You said Pete Slattery couldn't have tipped the cops because he was *dead*?"

"Early in the morning after the robbery Franklin buried him at the bottom of the hole that had been dug for the foundation of the new grandstand at Washington Field. It was the perfect place. The concrete footing for it was poured that very afternoon."

"Back up, please," I begged impatiently. "How did Franklin come to murder Slattery?"

"To understand that circumstance, you have to know about the relationship between Pete Slattery and Coach Franklin. In the terminology of today, Franklin was a closeted gay. Back then he would have been called a pansy, fruit, queer, and other colorful euphemisms for homosexual."

"Pete Slattery was also gay?"

"My guess is that Slattery went along with Franklin for money, as did the Perillo boys and Johnny Groover, eventually. I can only speculate. Because the Perillos wouldn't talk and Slattery and Johnny were dead, we had to take Coach Franklin at his word. But there was really no reason for him to lie about it. I suppose when you're facing two murder raps, plus complicity in an armed robbery, it doesn't matter admitting that you liked having sex with boys."

"Franklin confessed to everything?"

"Not at first, of course. But there weren't too many people who could stand up to being grilled by Tom Detwiler for very long. In fact, the only guy I know who did so was Johnny. Tom questioned him for six hours about the stickup and Johnny wouldn't break. If it hadn't been for that anonymous tip, they all would have gotten away with it. Some folks, such as Mrs. Perillo, believed Johnny confessed, and that for this he was given a break in the form of being allowed to enlist in the Marines, instead of going to prison."

"I don't understand. Since Johnny stood up to a grilling by Detwiler, and had paid for his role in the robbery by in effect pleading guilty by taking the judge's offer, why should Franklin think that Johnny was going to finally spill the beans, as you put it?"

"Two facts come into play here. Number one, Johnny had gone through what cynics of our day would call 'Meeting Jesus.' During the Second World War that phenomenon was known as a 'battlefield conversion.' Someone back then was quoted as saying, 'There are no atheists in foxholes.' Anyway, at the party in the gymnasium on that fateful night when Detwiler demanded that Johnny come in for more questioning, and Johnny agreed to do so, the coach overheard the conversation and was afraid Johnny would come clean at last."

"Franklin was afraid that Johnny would reveal Franklin's post-facto involvement?"

"Exactly."

"How did Johnny wind up dead on the football field?"

"Franklin said that after he left the party at the gym, he expected Johnny to drop in for a couple of drinks at Franklin's house with Franklin and Johnny's teammate, Richie Zale. When Johnny was a no-show, and after Richie went home, Franklin drove over to Johnny's house on the north side with the intention of talking to him. He'd assumed Johnny had gone home after the party. It was then about two o'clock and the Groover house was dark, except for a light in the downstairs hallway. Then a car pulled up and Johnny got out. When the car drove away, Franklin got out of his car and the two of them talked on the sidewalk. The upshot was that Johnny got in Franklin's car and they went out to the field house."

"If Johnny knew Franklin wanted to talk him out of seeing Detwiler, why on earth would Johnny agree to go?"

"The subject of Johnny's plan to see Detwiler never came up."

"Then why did he go?"

"I'm afraid that's an unanswerable question. Franklin wouldn't explain and Johnny was not around to tell us."

"What's your theory, if you have one?"

"According to Lieutenant Minetta, Johnny was drunk and feeling horny."

"You think Johnny went with for Franklin for sex? How does that jibe with Johnny's having had a meeting with Jesus?"

"The spirit is willing, but the flesh is weak?"

"Okay, so they arrive at the field house. Then what?"

"Maybe there was sex, maybe not. Franklin kept his mouth shut on that score, no pun intended. At some point Franklin brought up the matter of Johnny having a morning gabfest with Detwiler. Franklin found himself on the horns of a dilemma, which he solved by bashing Johnny with a dumbbell that Franklin used to keep in shape. He then confronted the timeless problem of the murderer."

"What to do with the body?"

"He couldn't leave it in the field house. And he was afraid to put it in the trunk of his car and take it out to the countryside to dump at some godforsaken spot. So he carried it out to the football field and left it on the fifty-yard line."

"What a stupid thing to do. Idiotic!"

"He was in a panic."

"Why did he kill Pete Slattery? Surely, he didn't expect Slattery to turn himself in and blow the whistle on him, too."

"Pete showed up to collect the money from the robbery. It had been stashed in a locker in Franklin's office where Franklin kept a few personal trophies, including Johnny Groover's old football uniform. It was Franklin's agreement to hold the loot until things cooled off that made him an accomplice after the fact. He felt that he had to go along, you see, because of the naughty things he'd been doing with Pete and the others."

"Slattery blackmailed him into stashing the loot? Why didn't he just hand it over?"

"Anyone who's been to the movies knows that the ugly reality of giving in to blackmail is that you don't know if that will end it."

"So he killed Slattery to foreclose the possibility of future blackmail. How could he be more stupid? Didn't he realize that he had as much on Slattery as Slattery had on him?"

"Back then, being accused of robbery was one thing," Scrappy said. "Being labeled queer was a different kettle of fish."

I smiled. "And there were fifty thousand dollars in the locker!"

"Funny thing about that money. It was still in the locker when Franklin confessed. After two years, more or less, he never helped himself to a single dollar."

"This man was even stupider than I thought."

"He'd also kept the pistol that Slattery had used in the robbery. It's what Franklin killed Slattery with."

"This is amazing. If Franklin had gone out to the football field right after the kids told him about finding a body, and then told the cops that Johnny Groover had been murdered, he might have gotten away with everything."

Now Scrappy smiled. "How could he know that Kate Fallon would be called in on the case? She died of a stroke a few years ago. She was quite a gal. You would have liked her. Everyone did. I miss her a lot. She used to visit me every week after I was condemned to live out my life in this place."

"What happened to Lieutenant Minetta?"

"He stayed in the Navy and served during the Korean War and Vietnam, then retired. He died about eight years ago with the rank of Rear Admiral."

"Aleck Whiteside?"

"Two weeks after all this Groover business when he was doing his weekly radio show, he slipped a note to an assistant in the studio that said, 'I am sick.' The assistant knew he had to be in dire straits, or he would have scribbled, 'I am *ill*.' He finished the broadcast, but died two hours later in a hospital of a massive heart attack. It happened the night before Aleck was to be at the White House to observe FDR present Johnny's posthumous Congressional Medal of Honor to Johnny's father. I think Aleck would have gotten a kick out of the irony."

"In going through the old newspapers," I said as I got off the bed, "I found nothing about Coach Franklin ever standing trial."

"That's because there wasn't one."

"Now can that be? He confessed to two murders."

"When we talked to him in the field house locker room, he was dressed in a sweat suit. He asked permission to change into street attire. Pete Slattery's gun was hidden in his clothes locker. Before Todd Doebling could grab it from his hand, the coach shot himself in the head. If you'd looked in the obituary pages of those old copies of the *Independence*, you'd have found his death notice. It gave the cause of his sudden demise as a heart attack. I wrote it myself."

"And for fifty years you covered up the truth."

"Yes, and now, my earnest acolyte in the temple of the First Amendment, I expect you to grant me and the memories of several fine people the favor of doing the same."

"You want me to ignore everything you've told me?"

"What would be the point in revealing all this now? There's no way for you to prove a word of what you'd write. All the participants are long gone, except me. I'll just deny it all and accuse you of making up your story because you were afraid you'd lose your job. Which of us do you think the people of Robinsville will believe? An ambitious, wet-behind-the-ears kid from out of town looking to make a name for himself at the cost of Robinsville's reputation? Or will they believe Scrappy MacFarland, a beloved character who has lived long enough to become a legend in his own time?"

"Now who's the blackmailer? What do you propose I tell my boss when I come back without a story?"

"Tell Paulie I'm out of cigars and I expect him to bring me an entire box when he comes out to see me so we can swap stories about his sister Kate."

EARLENE FOWLER

The Agatha Award-winning series featuring
Benni Harper, curator of San Celina's folk art museum
and amateur sleuth

FOOL'S PUZZLE   0-425-14545-X
Ex-cowgirl Benni Harper moved to San Celina, California, to begin a
new career as curator of the town's folk art museum. But when one
of the museum's first quilt exhibit artists is found dead, Benni must
piece together a pattern of family secrets and small-town lies to catch
the killer.

IRISH CHAIN   0-425-15137-9
When Brady O'Hara and his former girlfriend are murdered at the San
Celina Senior Citizen's Prom, Benni believes it's more than mere
jealousy—and she risks everything to unveil the conspiracy O'Hara
had been hiding for fifty years.

KANSAS TROUBLES   0-425-15696-6
After their wedding, Benni and Gabe visit his hometown near Wichita.
There Benni meets Tyler Brown: aspiring country singer, gifted
quilter, and former Amish wife. But when Tyler is murdered and the
case comes between Gabe and her, Benni learns that her marriage is
much like the Kansas weather: bound to be stormy.

GOOSE IN THE POND   0-425-16239-7
When Benni finds a dead woman lying facedown in the lake,
dressed in a Mother Goose costume, her investigation takes her
inside the Storyteller's Guild. There she discovers that Mother Goose
was telling more than fairy tales—she was a gossip columnist who
aired the kind of secrets that destroy lives—and inspire revenge...

SEVEN SISTERS   0-425-17917-6
When trying to unravel a feuding family's tragic past, Benni uncovers
a shocking pattern of tragedy—and stitches a hodgepodge of clues into
a very disturbing design.